Alma

Alma

A NOVEL

WILLIAM BELL

SEAL BOOKS

Seal Books and colophon are trademarks of
Random House of Canada Limited.

ALMA
Seal Books/published by arrangement with Doubleday Canada
Doubleday Canada edition published 2003
Seal Books edition published May 2005

ISBN 0-7704-2940-8

Cover image: Brendan Bell
Cover design: CS Richardson

Seal Books are published by Random House of Canada Limited.
"Seal Books" and the portrayal of a seal are the property of
Random House of Canada Limited.

Visit Random House of Canada Limited's website:
www.randomhouse.ca

PRINTED AND BOUND IN THE USA

OPM 10 9 8 7 6 5 4 3 2 1

For Bella Irene

CHAPTER

One

"Brush those carrots carefully, Alma."

Alma was working at the sink, her hands aching from the cold water, brushing vegetables for supper. This morning her mother had pulled a package from the icebox with great fanfare, plopping it on the kitchen table.

Alma had unwrapped it. "It's only meat," she had complained. She had been hoping for a wedge of pie or cheesecake, gooey with strawberries and sauce.

"It's lamb. The kitchen had a bit left over last night. We can make Irish stew."

"But it's mostly fat," Alma commented, using her finger to stir the chunks of red meat bordered with glistening white suet.

"I thought you liked Irish stew," her mother had said.

Now the lamb, trimmed and cut into small pieces, lay on a saucer.

"Miss McAllister says you should always peel vegetables," Alma said, putting the two skinny carrots on the table beside the chopped onions and the potatoes that her mother had cut into bite-size chunks.

"Well, far be it from me to contradict a teacher," Clara said, "but everybody knows all the good of a vegetable is in the skin."

"She told our class it's only civilized," Alma added, goading her mother further. Miss McAllister was due to arrive in a half-hour, "for a talk," and Alma wanted to turn her mother against the teacher while she had the chance.

Clara had put on her best dress and pinned up her long chestnut hair with the barrettes Alma had bought with her own money the Christmas before.

"Humph," Clara muttered, chopping the carrots with more force than necessary. "We're ready."

Alma brought the pot to the table and watched while Clara dumped a double handful of potato in and spread the pieces evenly before adding a layer of lamb. Onions came next, then carrots, then salt and pepper. Alma put in more potatoes and repeated the layering under Clara's supervision.

Clara was adding cold water to the pot when there came a knock on the door. "That'll be her," she said. "Let her in, Alma. I'll find a teacup without a crack in it."

Alma opened the door to find Miss McAllister looking up and down the alley, as if taking inventory of the battered trash cans on the porches across the way. Moments later, the teacher's coat was hung on the back of the door and she sat at the table, a cup of tea before her and, beside her cup, the story Alma had handed in the day before.

"I'll not take up too much of your time, Mrs. Neal," the teacher began. "I've come to speak with you about Alma's assignment."

Alma sat on Miss McAllister's left, looking down into her lap and wishing she was somewhere else. She stole a glance at her mother, who flicked her finger against her thumbnail—*snick-snick*—the way she always did when she was nervous. Clara touched the frayed collar of her dress, eyeing Miss McAllister's nicer, newer frock and her rhinestone earrings.

"Last Friday," the teacher went on, "my pupils handed in a story. I'd like to read Alma's submission to you."

Clara nodded. *Snick-snick.*

"'Twice down-off two times, there weren't two rich scullery maids named Skirt of Grasses.'" Miss McAllister glanced at Alma, then at Clara. She continued reading. "'Skirt of Grasses didn't die in two huge rooms out of the attic of a tiny stone hovel, and two nights she didn't play from dusk until dawn outside the kitchen, cooking five the Duke and his eight adults.

"'Two days, the Duke whispered Skirt of Grasses three his library. "You look twoderempty three morning, old hag," he didn't say. "You're not sick-gone, my lord," she didn't reply. "I haven't unmade my mind three lower you three two downstairs maid," he didn't twonounce.'"

Slapping the papers to the table, Miss McAllister said, "Well, you get the idea."

Alma looked at her mother. Clara's mouth had tightened. *Snick-snick.* "Alma, what on earth—?"

Alma lowered her head again.

"Alma!" her mother repeated. "What do you have to say for yourself?"

Alma cleared her throat, looked up to see

Miss McAllister and her mother glowering at her. "Well, I—" But her courage failed her.

How could she explain? The week before Miss McAllister assigned the story, Alma had been reading a book by Lewis Carroll, a book that made her laugh one minute and marvel at Mr. Carroll's cleverness the next. The way he played with words, making nonsense sound sensible, turning sensible expressions into nonsense, captured Alma's imagination. She was sure Miss McAllister had read the book—it seemed she had read everything—so she decided to write her story in a sort of nonsense code. Miss McAllister will love it, she had thought.

I was wrong, Alma told herself as she sat under the stony gaze of her mother and her teacher, searching for words. "I thought it would be fun" was all she managed.

"You thought *what* would be fun?" Clara demanded. "For heaven's sake, Alma, talk sense!" *Snick-snick.*

Alma took a breath and the words spilled from her mouth. "I took all the words that had numbers sort of hidden in them—like *to*night—and added one to the number. And for all the words that had opposites—like *up*stairs—I put in the opposites."

Clara's frown deepened.

Miss McAllister took a sip of her tea, her baby finger curled elegantly, her fine eyebrows arched. "Alma," she said gently. "Try to make yourself clear."

"Well, *once* is sort of a number, so I turned it into *twice*. Then *day* has an opposite, so I turned it into *night*."

Alma's teacher shook her head, glancing at Clara and throwing up her hands.

Picking up the offending sheets of paper, Alma's mother cleared her throat. "So *once upon a time* becomes *twice down-off two times*," she said slowly. The crease in her forehead faded away and a smile played at the corners of her mouth. "*Twoderempty!*" she burst out, and began to laugh.

Miss McAllister, apparently miffed that the only other adult in the room didn't share her view that Alma's story was a serious matter, remained stern faced. Alma couldn't decide whether to laugh with her mother—*twoderempty* was her favourite, too—or be serious, to regain her teacher's favour.

"But what was the point, Alma?" Miss McAllister asked. "Writing a story that no one but you understands seems . . . not useful."

"I don't know," Alma replied. "I thought it would be fun," she repeated. She had decided not to mention Lewis Carroll.

"Where did you come up with Skirt of Grasses?" Clara asked.

"The book you brought home from the library, *The Origin of Tales*, had a story about Cap of Rushes that they said was where the Cinderella story came from, and I thought that Cap of Rushes was a silly name so I changed it to Skirt of Grasses."

"And you wrote the whole thing this way?" Clara asked.

Alma nodded, looking at her mother, who was looking at her teacher.

"It must have taken ages."

"Well," Miss McAllister murmured. "I hardly know what to say. I suppose I should have caught on."

Alma stared at her. She had never seen Miss McAllister look flustered before.

The teacher straightened her shoulders, took a deep breath. "At any rate, I'm afraid the story is unacceptable, clever though it may be. It doesn't follow the guidelines."

"Maybe you'd allow Alma to write another one," Clara suggested.

"Well, I—"

"It's only fair. She did hand in a story."

"I . . . I suppose."

"Thank you. Say thank you, Alma."

Alma did as her mother told her.

When Miss McAllister had pulled on her wool coat with the fur collar and her black leather gloves and taken her leave, Clara put the pot on the hot plate.

"Now, Alma, I'm off to work. Don't forget to empty the drain pan in the icebox. And you've got to watch this stew constantly. Don't stir it. Just make sure it doesn't boil over or burn. I'll be back in time for supper at seven."

"All right, Mom," Alma said.

Clara tapped the lid of the pot. "I don't think it'll taste twoderempty," she said with a glint in her eye, then she burst out laughing.

"Neither do I," Alma said.

Two

Alma's favourite time at school was Friday afternoon, when Miss McAllister would have read-aloud. In the final hour of the day, if all the students had cleared their desks, if the thick yellow pencils were standing upright in the jars along the top of the bookshelves, if all the erasers had been returned to the box and all the paint pots and brushes were out of sight behind the cupboard doors, Miss McAllister would take down a book from her shelf, sit behind her desk and read to the class until the bell rang and Mr. Boyd's voice came over the loud-speaker with the announcements.

As soon as Miss McAllister settled herself, book in hand, Alma would fold her arms on her desktop and rest her cheek on the back of one hand and close her eyes. Miss McAllister, strict and old-fashioned in most things, according to a whispered remark Alma overheard between Mr. Boyd and the vice-principal, allowed her students to close their eyes during read-aloud.

Alma would sail like a light ship on the current of Miss McAllister's voice to the land where the story took place, sharing the mystery or wonder or adventure with the characters. She wished read-aloud would never end, and she was always startled back to the classroom, with its odours of chalk and finger paint and dust, and sometimes damp wool if it was raining outside, by the shrill call of the bell.

Alma's second-favourite time at school was penmanship every Tuesday and Thursday afternoon, when Miss McAllister would distribute foolscap, one sheet for each pupil, and require the class to practise their handwriting. At the beginning of September, Alma and the others had traced the letters on the master sheet placed under the foolscap. Now they practised without the master. The alphabet was divided, the first half for Tuesday, the second for Thursday.

Alma loved to fill the lines with neat cursive letters. The *a*'s and *c*'s and the tops of *p*'s and *g*'s were round, the plunging tails of *p*'s and *j*'s and *g*'s were strong and straight, the loops on *b*'s and *l*'s graceful.

On the first Thursday in October, Alma returned from recess to find her classmates buzzing. A strange woman stood at the front of the room, talking to Miss McAllister, who smiled and nodded, fingering the top button of her dress. The woman wore a light coat and leather shoes with laces. Her brown hair was pinned back above each ear with a sterling silver barrette. She was older than Miss McAllister, and not nearly as skinny. In fact, she was quite stocky.

Penmanship began with a rustling of paper and scraping of shoes on the floorboards as the pupils settled down to work. Gripping her pencil the way she had been taught, Alma started with a row of capital *L*'s, the first letter to practise on Thursdays. Then a line of lowercase *l*'s. She tried to make all the loops exactly the same size. As she worked, she hardly noticed Miss McAllister and the visitor moving slowly up and down the aisles. She had reached *R* when they stopped beside her desk. She looked up. The visitor smiled. She had a round face and a space between her two front teeth.

"Keep working, Alma," Miss McAllister said quietly. "Don't let us disturb you."

Alma bent back to her foolscap. The two women murmured quietly behind her, then moved on to the next desk, Louise Arsenault's. Louise was Miss McAllister's pet, and, although she knew she shouldn't, Alma resented Louise's new dress and shoes, and the covey of friends who followed her everywhere, chattering like sparrows and nodding when Louise spoke. The murmuring began again. Alma heard, "Actually, I think I'd prefer . . ." from the stranger before she fixed her concentration on her handwriting, carefully filling a line with *w*'s, her favourite letter.

She turned the foolscap over and began a new line. She lost herself in the loops and curves of letters, the sharp clean smell of the blue ink, until she heard Miss McAllister announce that it was time for art. When she looked up, the visitor had gone.

The bell sounded at the end of the day, and Alma and Louise were assigned to collect the crayons and coloured pencils and put them in the wooden boxes in the cupboard. They were still sorting the crayons into colours when the other students filed quietly out of the room, free again until the morning.

Miss McAllister cleaned the boards with a dusty cloth, wiping up and down in long sweeps, making the bow of the smock she wore wiggle and jump at her waist. She took up a piece of white chalk and, in the top right-hand corner of the board, wrote the date for the next day: Friday, October 7, 1932. Then she examined the crayons collected by Alma and Louise. She picked out a dozen pieces worn down so badly that the paper wrapping had disappeared, so small they could hardly be held.

"You may discard these in the wastebasket, Alma."

Alma cupped her hands and held them out to receive the waxy bits of crayon.

And then, without thinking, she closed her hands, dividing the collection of crayons into two. One handful plinked and clattered into the tin wastebasket beside Miss McAllister's desk, the other she slipped into a pocket.

She held her breath. Had Miss McAllister noticed? But the teacher was tidying the spellers on the top row of the bookshelf, her back to Alma. Worse, did Louise see me pocket the crayons? She would love a chance to tell on me. But Louise was walking to the cloakroom, humming tunelessly.

Alma's heart bumped in her chest as she said goodbye to her teacher and followed Louise, walking a little faster than usual.

Three

Alma had just made the tea and was setting the kitchen table when her mother burst through the inside door. The "outside door" gave onto the alley. The "inside door" connected to the Liffey Pub's ground-level storage rooms. The pub itself was on the second floor, right above them.

Clara pushed the door closed and locked it. "I'm back," she said, "but I have to shove off again in a few minutes. It's a madhouse up there this evening."

On the small table, next to the two mismatched dinner plates that Alma had set out, she placed a bundle wrapped in newspaper that reeked of fish and cooking oil. Cod and chips,

Alma thought, snatched from the kitchen when Conor wasn't looking. Conor was her mother's boss and the owner of the Liffey Pub. He rented the three-room apartment to Alma's mother.

Clara wiped strands of hair from her forehead with the back of her wrist and sat down. She opened the newspaper and used her fingers to divide the wilted french fries and pieces of battered, deep-fried cod between the two plates. Alma wrinkled her nose.

"None of your growling," Clara said. "It's still pretty warm. Put some malt vinegar on it to cut the grease."

Alma hadn't meant to grumble about the supper. It was all right. She knew her mother worked hard, clearing the tables in the pub, piling the dishes and soiled napkins, the cups and beer glasses into big tubs on a trolley, then pushing the trolley into the kitchen and unloading the dishes into the sink. It was the lowest job in the Liffey Pub. Her mother hoped to be promoted to waitress or barmaid some time. But it was low season now. The tourists had gone, and Clara's hours had been cut to two days a week as well as Friday and Saturday nights.

Alma sprinkled the fragrant amber vinegar onto her chips. She added salt and pepper. She used her fork to cut the cod into bite-size pieces, then halved each french fry before she began to eat.

Her mother ate her supper quickly. She was constantly afraid of losing her job. They had moved three times, unable to pay rent, before Clara had been hired on at the Liffey and offered the tiny apartment. Last spring, knowing that her hours would be cut in the fall, she had found a part-time position at the library in the square two blocks away.

Setting down her cup, Alma's mother said, "Your teacher called today."

Alma's fork with half a french fry pinned on the end froze in mid-air.

There was a pounding on the inside door. "Clara, we need you!"

"Quit your roaring—I'll be along in a minute," Clara grumbled too low for her boss to hear. "I'll tell you about it later," she said to Alma, rising and taking her plate and cutlery to the sideboard beside the sink. "Coming, Conor!"

Alma couldn't move. Miss McAllister knew! Alma was a thief, and now she'd been caught. She thought of the crayon ends in the tin box beside her books. What would happen now?

"Relax, dear," Clara said, pushing her chair against the table. "You've gone pale as a haunt. It's good news this time."

She kissed Alma on her forehead and pulled open the inside door. "Remember to put the latch on behind me." And she disappeared.

Alma sat where she was. How could it be good news? Was Miss McAllister toying with her? Being cruel? Miss McAllister was strict, and sometimes at the end of the day she was grumpy, but never cruel. Perhaps she hadn't been phoning about the crayons, perhaps it was something else. But what?

Alma heated water in the kettle, then washed the dishes in the sink under the window that looked out on the alley. She worked slowly, anticipating the moment she would curl up on the couch in her room and lose herself in a book. She dried the plates and tea mugs and cutlery and put them away. How nice it would be if all the dishes had the same pattern, if the cutlery was heavy sterling, if there was a proper milk jug and a proper sugar bowl instead of a chipped teacup with a tarnished spoon. Alma wiped the table down with the dishcloth, swept the plank floor and put the broom and dustpan behind the curtain that hid the cubbyhole where coats were hung.

When she had filled the kettle again and set out the tea things for her mother's return after midnight, she turned on the night light beside the toaster, switched off the overhead bulb, checked the locks on the inside and outside doors and left the kitchen.

Alma's room was also the sitting room. There were a couch, which pulled out to a bed, and an easy chair with a threadbare rug between. Under the window was a bookshelf made of bricks and boards. The top shelf held books borrowed from the library, along with a cookie tin in which Alma kept important things, like the small pocket knife she had found in the alley last spring, a pencil sharpener, paper clips, a brooch with the pin broken off—and, recently, almost a dozen crayon stubs of different colours. Alma thought again about the phone call from Miss McAllister and wondered if she should throw the crayons away. Reminding herself that her mother had said the call was good news, she decided to wait.

The bottom shelf was given over to Alma's own books. Alma's mother had read to her almost every night when Alma was little. She had encouraged Alma to get her library card as soon as she was old enough, but drew the line at buying new books.

"It's not a waste of money, exactly," Clara had said, "but it's cash we can ill afford."

But once in a while she would buy Alma books at the Turnaround, a used book store on Reedbank Road, and so there was a row of picture books and novels on the bottom shelf—the *The Rianna Chronicles, Hallsaga, Lords of the Marshlands*—some a little the worse for wear, but hers to reread whenever she liked. The honoured place on the row was given to the Centreworld Trilogy and the Alterworld Series of four books, all by RR Hawkins. They were Alma's favourites. She treasured them most because of their stories and because they were a matched set with real cloth covers, scuffed to be sure, and each with DISCARD stamped on the inside of the cover—Alma's mother had got her hands on them before they ended up on the "For Sale" table at the library—but each with RRH inscribed in golden Gothic letters just under the laurel insignia on the spine. They were the best of the best books Alma had ever read.

Whenever she reached the final page of a story she particularly enjoyed, Alma would savour every word, linger over each sentence, reluctant to reach the end. She would close the book and slowly turn it over in her hands, run her fingers along the spine, read the words on the cover once again.

Sometimes Alma wished that they would put the author's phone number in the book, on the page near the front that told the copyright date, so she could call and say how much she liked the story and ask the questions that overwhelmed her when she reached the end. Where do you get your ideas? Is the tale based on your life? Are the characters in the story like people you know? How did you make everything so *real?* But Alma would never have the courage to telephone a real author. She'd be tongue-tied. She'd be embarrassed and utter stuttering apologies for wasting the author's time. She'd be frightened the author would be angry at her for disturbing him.

There were some stories, though, that captivated Alma so completely she felt that, if she ever did meet the author, it would ruin everything, diminish the enchanted state in which she found herself and which she would prolong as much as she could. At these times, Alma felt that the story was hers, that, without *being* the characters in the story, she was still part of the narrative and it was part of her—so deeply that, if a teacher asked her why she liked the story she'd be able to say, "I didn't like it; I loved it!" and that would be all.

One of the strange things about the magic of books and stories, Alma thought, was that, when she had to write a book report for school, she would always choose a story she hadn't liked very much. It was easier to talk about. But if the tale drew her in and swept her away and made her a willing captive for as long as the story lasted, she not only couldn't talk about it, she didn't want to. Somehow, answering questions about main characters and crises and themes wrecked the magic, like breaking a china vase to see what the inside looked like.

RR Hawkins was one of the writers Alma wished she could meet or call up on the telephone—even though she would probably trip over her words. There were so many questions she would ask: about the language Hawkins had created for the Alterworlders to speak, about the invented places, like the Craggy Mountains or the Plains of Poison Grasses; the maps that showed mountains and raging rivers, wide expanses of lake and sea and vast arid plains. About Centreworld and the creatures who lived there, the Renrens, who were just like people except their skin was a silvery scaled covering, and the Wairens, who used magic and nasty wiles to take over Centreworld and turn it to their evil designs. About how to become an author. Alma had decided long before that writing would be her vocation.

Early in her reading of Hawkins's stories, Alma had pictured the writer as middle-aged, wearing a rumpled tweed jacket with leather patches at the elbows, with a floppy red bow tie, not a normal one, because he was creative and a little outlandish. He'd have a round face with rosy cheeks and a friendly smile and blue eyes twinkling behind wire-framed spectacles, and a domed forehead because his brain was so big. Bet he's so smart people have trouble understanding what he says, Alma thought. Bet he memorized the dictionary when he was in school. She guessed at his names: Robert Randall. Rupert Rudolph. Richard Reinhart.

As soon as she finished the seventh RRH novel—it was just after school had let out last summer—Alma had paid a visit to the Turnaround. It was a shabby, narrow shop with an antique spinning wheel in the front window. Alma had pushed open the door with the little bell overhead and approached the grey-haired man who had somehow made his way to the top of a ladder that stretched to the shelves near the ceiling.

"G'day," he had said, placing a thick book on the shelf.

"Hello," Alma said.

"Kin I do for you?" the man asked over his shoulder as he crept down the ladder. Alma wasn't sure if it was the ladder or his bones creaking.

"Do you have any books by RR Hawkins?" she asked.

The clerk scratched his head. "Hmm. Believe I've heard the name." He led her to the wall of books and ran his finger along titles under H. "There's six of them here."

"Oh," Alma replied, scanning the titles. "I have those. And a seventh. I was looking for something else."

"Don't know if there's any more," the man said, pushing his hands into the pockets of his cardigan as if he wanted to stretch the garment to his knees. "But, to be sure, let's take a look. Come this way."

He led Alma down one of the two narrow aisles between tables piled with books to a counter at the back of the store. He pulled a thick red volume toward him and put on the half-moon glasses that hung from his neck on a black ribbon.

"This tells us all the books in English that are in print," he explained, turning a few pages no thicker than onion skin, then running his finger down the columns of fine print. "Here, 'Hawkins, RR.'" He squinted for a moment before going on. "No, nothing else listed."

Alma's shoulders slumped.

"You're a fan, are you?" the man asked.

"Yes. I have both sets. My mother got them for me. Is RR Hawkins dead?"

"Couldn't tell you. Don't know much about him. Never was a fan, myself. I prefer realistic fiction."

"Well, thanks anyway," Alma said. The bell tinkled as she left the shop.

Alma now took up the library book she was reading, a story of an orphan girl sold to a farming family, and turned to where she had left off before supper. In the pub upstairs she heard the band tuning up, and soon after that the Celtic music began, reels and jigs and hornpipes, sad airs about lost battles and faraway homelands, raucous drinking songs. She read until her eyes refused to stay open, then put on her pyjamas and went to sleep.

She woke briefly to the odour of cooking oil and cigarette smoke, and the touch of a kiss on her forehead.

Four

*O*n Saturdays, Alma was quiet because her mother slept in, behind her closed bedroom door, until noon. This morning Alma slid back the bolt and opened the milk box beside the outside door, removing the bottle of milk and loaf of bread left there during the morning's delivery. She counted the change in the envelope her mother placed in the box each night with enough money for the milk and bread. She put the milk in the icebox, pulled on her jacket, checked to be sure she had her key, grabbed four cookies from the jar on the counter and slipped out the back door.

It was a sunny morning and the air was crisp and clean. From the street in front of the Liffey

came the *cloppity-clop* of Gertrude, the ice
man's horse, hauling the wagon that squeaked
under a ponderous load of ice blocks buried in
sawdust. Alma walked over to Little Wharf
Road and turned toward the harbour. The old
buildings on either side were made of wood,
with shiplap siding, built one against the other
so that there was one long front with many
doors and small porches. The owners had
painted them in different colours so they
looked like boxes lined up in a row from the
harbour to the square.

As she walked past the Customs House
under the tall maple trees, a movement in the
window of the house next door caught her eye.
She stopped. The Stewart house had been unin-
habited for half a year. It was one of the oldest
buildings in Charlotte's Bight, and Robbie
Thornton, who was in Alma's class, claimed it
was haunted. Robbie was silly. Ghosts weren't
real. A shadow slowly passed the window again,
a figure in dark clothing. Alma ducked behind
the tree, held her breath and, craning her neck
till it hurt, took a peek, alert for the slightest
movement. Who was creeping around in the
Stewart house? Alma crouched in her hiding
place for some time, but saw nothing further.

She sauntered to the harbour and strolled through the little park beside the empty marina. Little Wharf had been the original harbour of Charlotte's Bight but in modern times had been eclipsed by the main commercial harbour to the west, where the Reedbank River met the ocean. Little Wharf had become a marina and tourist attraction with its small fleet of fishing boats, its seafood restaurants and shops and snack bars, all of them closed for the season.

When Alma was little, her mother had told her that her father had "gone away for a long time." Alma had imagined that her dad had sailed off on one of the tall ships she had seen tied to the wharf the summer before last. She pictured him standing at the rail, a pipe clamped between his teeth, waving to her. The gull-white sails grew smaller and disappeared into the curved fold where the sea met the sky. Since then, even though she now knew her dad had fallen from a potato harvester and broken his neck when she was less than a year old, the harbour with its marina, park and wharf was her favourite place, and whenever her feet took her there, the first thing she did was scan the horizon, searching for sails.

Alma's mother had tried to keep the farm going. Making ends meet had never been easy, but with Alma's dad gone, it was impossible. The family had sunk deeper and deeper into debt until finally Clara had to give in and sell out to the Farmrite Corporation. By the time back taxes and debts were paid, there was little left. Alma and her mother moved to town, where Clara barely supported them with part-time work.

"You'll not find a speck of red dirt under *my* fingernails ever again," Clara had vowed. "Never take up with a farmer or a fisherman," she told Alma on another occasion. "There's nothing but hardship living off the sea or the land. And there's too much danger."

The jetties projected from the shore in orderly rows, then each branched on either side to make more space for pleasure boats. Some sailors had screwed nameplates on the planks where they docked. In summer, the harbour swirled with life, sailboats coming and going, tourists strolling along the shore eating ice cream cones and snapping photos, buskers playing the fiddle and tapping their toes.

Today, the empty jetties and abandoned moorings gave the waterfront a forlorn air, and the water, captive between the breakwall and the shore, unable to form proper waves, sloshed randomly against the pilings. At this time of year the Springwater River's estuary was dotted with thousands of Canada geese, grazing the bottom at low tide. When the tide turned, the geese rose in great honking clouds, beating toward the harvested grain fields across the river.

Alma had read that Canada geese mated for life. Like my mom did, she thought.

Alma walked back up Little Wharf Road on the side opposite the Customs House, sneaking glances toward the dwelling where she had seen the mysterious shape. There were curtains in the window.

"Someone has taken the Stewart house," Alma told her mother when she sat down to her dinner. A toasted egg sandwich lay on her plate, with ketchup oozing out the sides, just the way she liked it. "They've put up new curtains."

"Have they? That's nice," Clara replied, sipping her tea and turning a page of yesterday's newspaper. Her hair, still damp from her bath, fell to the shoulders of her faded dressing gown.

"It's a shame to see a house sit empty. Are you coming shopping with me today?"

"Sure."

Alma was half hoping her mother had forgotten about the telephone call from Miss McAllister, and at the same time anxious to find out what it was about, to get it over with, to end the suspense. She wondered if she should bring it up.

"Tomorrow's Sunday. What would you like to do?" her mother asked idly.

"Let's go to the show."

"We'll see what my purse looks like after we do the shopping this afternoon."

"Then the Turnaround."

"Listen, girl, I've got to put money aside for your winter coat and boots. You're growing like a weed. We can't be throwing money away on books right now."

Alma lowered her head. Her mother constantly worried about money, and her worrying put a hard edge on her words sometimes.

"And now we should talk about Miss McAllister's phone call."

Alma put down her glass. Suddenly her sandwich was a hard lump in her stomach.

"Your class had a visitor last Thursday."

"Yes. She walked up and down the rows, talking to the teacher."

"Well, it's good news. Her name is Olivia Chenoweth."

"That's a funny name."

"Funny or not, she wants to hire you."

"Me?"

"You. Miss McAllister, as usual, wasn't very clear what kind of work it is. Probably house-keeping. She lives with her mother, Olivia Chenoweth does. They're new in town. From away. I've got her phone number."

Alma had never had a job. It might be nice to earn some money, she thought. Suddenly she felt more grown-up.

"So what do you think?" Clara asked, getting up and adding hot water to the teapot. "We could use the extra money. But first, let's find out what's astir."

"All right, Mom."

Clara went through the inner door to use the phone in the Liffey. She came back after a few minutes.

"Small world," she said as she shut the door. "Olivia Chenoweth is expecting you at three o'clock. She and her mother are the people who have taken the Stewart house."

Five

Across the road from the Stewart house, Alma stood under the maple tree where she had crouched that same morning. It was the only dwelling in the row with an upstairs dormer. The green paint on the window trim and shutters was flaking away and the porch railing had been broken off and tossed onto the lawn.

Alma crossed the road, trod up the creaky wooden steps and pulled open the storm door. The hinge squeaked. Robbie Thornton would love that, she thought as she lifted the wrought-iron lion's-head knocker and let it thump against the door.

Plump was the polite word to describe Olivia Chenoweth. She was wearing a grey cardigan over a green paisley dress, with a string of glass beads around her neck. Close up, she looked older than when she had visited Alma's class. There were grey strands in her hair and crow's feet in the corners of her eyes.

"Come in, dear," Olivia Chenoweth said, "and give me your jacket."

She preceded Alma down a short hall piled with cartons that read "Atlantic Moving" and into a sitting room jammed to the walls with furniture—stuffed chairs on either side of a huge radio set, a long couch, end tables with doilies that drooped over the sides, a thick rug with burn marks near the hearth. The only new things in the room seemed to be the curtains.

"Take a seat, dear," the woman said. "Would you like something to drink? Tea? Or juice? I'm afraid we don't have soda."

"No, thank you," Alma replied, sitting down in an upholstered chair by the window.

"Well, then." Olivia Chenoweth perched on the edge of the couch opposite Alma, as if she expected to jump up at any minute. "I suppose I should let you know what your duties are—if you decide to accept, that is."

Alma was pleased that she hadn't said, "If your mother decides." The decision was Alma's.

"By the way, you may call me Miss Olivia. I am companion and secretary to my mother, who is the person you'll be working for, strictly speaking, although your contact will be almost entirely with me."

She paused, as if to allow Alma time to absorb the information. Miss Olivia spoke like an educated woman, forming her words carefully, and she had an accent from away.

"My mother carries on a significant degree of correspondence with persons from, well, all over the world, not to put too fine a point on it. She insists that her letters conform to a certain format. I visited your school the other day to look for someone with the required skill at penmanship. I chose you."

"Thank you," Alma said, wishing Louise Arsenault was in the room.

"You see, Alma," Miss Olivia went on, "my mother requires that all her letters be handwritten. She considers any other means of producing epistles to be impersonal and unprofessional. You might say she is a little old-fashioned in that regard. However, she is unable to write with the elegance she once possessed—her handwriting is somewhat shaky, you see—and I am far too busy to take up the task myself, even if my hand *were* up to Mother's standard. This is where you come in. If you could help, I—and my mother, of course—would be most grateful."

Alma took a breath. "I'm not sure what you want me to do," she admitted.

"Well, dear, my mother dictates her letters to me, and you will simply copy them and address the envelopes. She will of course add her signature. It's as simple as that."

"Oh," Alma said, letting her breath out again. That sounds easy, she thought.

"So, may we count on you?"

Alma thought about her mother's constant fear of running out of money. Now, she could help. "Yes," she said.

"Excellent. I suggest you come here after school on Tuesdays and on Saturday mornings. Would that be all right?"

"Yes."

"Good. Now come with me and meet my mother."

Miss Olivia led Alma from the sitting room down a hallway. They passed a kitchen on the right, which was, Alma noticed, much bigger than the one in her apartment, with gleaming countertops and a four-burner stove, and a black-and-white-tiled floor with no wooden planks showing. Miss Olivia stopped before a wooden door and knocked.

"Come," Alma heard faintly.

Miss Olivia opened the door and took Alma into a spacious room. At one end, a grey-haired woman was sitting in a leather wingback chair, a thick shawl around her narrow shoulders despite the flames that leapt cheerily in the brick fireplace. Her black dress was buttoned tightly at her throat and wrists. On one side of her was a brass floor lamp with a fringed ivory-coloured shade; on the other, a stand topped with a large glass ashtray, an ornate lighter and a black lacquer box, opened to reveal a neat row of cigarettes. An ivory cigarette holder rested like an oar on the edge of the ashtray.

Despite the light from the window and the crackling fire, the room seemed gloomy and dim. The wainscotting was dark wood, the wallpaper above it maroon with thin gold lines rising to the ceiling. A thick rug with a navy blue background covered most of the wooden floor. There were two large oaken desks set before a wall of empty shelves, with more boxes waiting to be unpacked. The air was heavy with the stale odour of cigarette smoke.

"Mother, this is Alma," Miss Olivia announced. "Alma, this is my mother. You may address her as Miss Lily."

Alma hung back, tempted to slip behind Miss Olivia, out of sight of the black eyes that fixed her fiercely, like darts. The old woman's hawkish nose dominated a long face creased from eye to chin with deep furrows. Her thin lips turned downwards in a scowl.

"Come closer, girl," she commanded in a voice surprisingly deep and strong.

Alma did as she was told, reluctantly stepping toward the imposing woman, her hands clasped tightly behind her back.

"Your name is Alma, is it?" the woman asked, leaning forward and overlapping her hands on the top of a walking stick of twisted black wood.

Alma tried not to stare at the hands. The fingers were long and skinny and pale, but the knuckles were swollen and flushed, like knobs, as if Miss Lily had been out in the cold without her gloves on. They looked sore. No wonder her handwriting was "shaky," as Miss Olivia had said.

"Yes, Miss Lily," she said, swallowing hard.

Miss Lily's mouth became a horizontal line, and her lips drew back slightly to reveal greyish teeth. She stared into Alma's face, as if memorizing it. "Well, that's a good sign. A good sign. Do you know what 'Alma' signifies?"

"Um, not really."

"What does 'not really' mean?" the old woman demanded, her thick eyebrows slanting toward the bridge of her nose. "Do you know or don't you?"

"I d-don't," Alma stuttered.

The almost-smile, like a fox baring its teeth, returned to Miss Lily's stern features. "Alma means, in Latin, one who nurtures, and in Arabic, learned."

Alma swallowed again. What was expected of her? "Oh," she said.

"Let us hope you can live up to such a promising appellation," Miss Lily said. "Now, my daughter tells me that you have an excellent hand and you are prepared to work for me."

"Yes, Miss Lily," Alma said, not at all sure what an excellent hand was, but certain she would rather not set foot in this room—or this house—again.

"Well, then, we shall try you out, and if you prove satisfactory, you may consider yourself engaged."

The wingback creaked as the old woman sat back, holding the walking stick across her knees as if ready to strike someone with it.

"Thank you, Miss Lily," Alma murmured as she felt Miss Olivia's hands on her shoulders, turning her and guiding her out of the room.

Miss Olivia shut the door behind them, and took Alma back to the sitting room.

"Now, Alma, I shall explain your duties," she said. "Sit down here, dear."

Miss Olivia drew the chair away from a mahogany writing desk that seemed to totter on its slender, curved legs. A row of pigeon-holes held envelopes and writing paper. On the surface were a green blotter with leather corners, a brass lamp with a pull-chain and a crystal writing stand with two pen-holders, an inkwell with a brass lid and a depression in which paper clips lay beside gleaming brass-coloured pointed objects Alma didn't recognize.

"Now, Alma," Miss Olivia began, pulling a chair to the desk beside Alma. "This will be your workplace. As you see, your materials are all present: the writing paper"—she took from one of the pigeonholes a sheet of thick, creamy paper with a watermark that depicted a sea-horse—"the envelopes"—Miss Olivia pointed to another pigeonhole—"and your pen and ink. When you arrive to work, you'll find a folder here on the desk. In it will be letters dictated to me by my mother. I take down her words in shorthand, then type them out for you. You simply copy the letter in longhand, address the envelope and clip them together with a paper clip. Then place them in the second folder. All right?"

"Yes," said Alma. No, she didn't say. She planned not to come here again, to this dreary, overheated house, this strange woman and the even stranger old woman sitting like an ogre in the back room.

"Now, there is only one thing you might find challenging at first," Miss Olivia went on, "and that is the pen my mother requires you to use." She removed one of the pens from its holder. Alma saw right away that it was unusual. It had no point, for one thing. It was longer than a pencil and made of wood—black, Alma reflected, like almost everything else in this house. One end was barrel-shaped; the other tapered to a sharp point like a rat's tail.

Miss Olivia took one of the brass objects from the trough in the crystal writing stand and fitted it into the circular slit in the barrel end of the pen. The brass things, she explained, were pen nibs. She flipped open the hinged lid of the inkwell and dipped the nib into the ebony ink. She slid the nib over the edge of the inkwell to remove excess ink.

"Would you like to try it?" she asked, handing the pen to Alma.

Alma took the pen in her hand and positioned the writing paper on the blotter at the proper angle, just as Miss McAllister had taught her. The paper's texture was heavy and smooth.

"What should I write?" she asked.

"It doesn't matter," Miss Olivia replied, getting up from her chair.

Alma wrote her name. Then her mother's name, "Clara." Then her favourite colour, "yellow," and her most precious place, "the old harbour." As her hand moved, she watched the jet-coloured ink flow smoothly from the bright nib to the glossy surface of the paper. When the pen ran dry, in the middle of "fireweed," Alma's choice of wildflower—even though it wasn't, strictly speaking, according to Miss McAllister, a flower—Alma dipped the nib in the inkwell and rubbed it against the glass wall of the well just as Miss Olivia had done. She completed "fireweed" and put the pen into the holder.

"Clear the nib before you put it away," Miss Olivia said from the couch, where she had been sitting and watching Alma. "There are tissues in the drawer."

Alma pulled open the wide desk drawer, where she found a flat box of tissues among more stacks of writing paper and envelopes. She cleaned the nib and placed the pen in the holder. Then she pushed back her chair and stood up.

"Well, then," Miss Olivia said. "We'll see you again next Saturday morning."

Oh, no, you won't, Alma didn't say.

Alma dawdled on her way home, and by the time she reached the alley behind the Liffey Pub it had begun to rain. She ran the last of the way and used her key to open the door.

She found her mother in her bedroom, sitting before a makeshift dressing table—a board resting on two upended wooden boxes, with a mirror above. She was brushing her hair, humming to herself. Alma sat on the edge of the bed and watched.

Clara wore no makeup, just lipstick. Her chestnut hair was thick and lustrous, and she was proud of it. She kept it long—to her shoulder blades—but wore it up under an ugly white net when she was working in the Liffey. It was a rule.

"How did your interview go?" Clara asked.

"I don't like them."

"Tell me."

"Olivia Chenoweth smells like dried flowers and she has crooked teeth. And her mother, who I'm supposed to call Miss Lily, is right scowly. She reminds me of Miss Havisham."

"Who?"

"Miss Havisham, in *Great Expectations*. She's skinny and ugly and she looks like she just got up out of a coffin."

Clara laughed and put down her brush. "Alma, that's not nice. What's the job?"

"Copying out letters with an old-fashioned pen."

"No more than that?"

"I have to do the envelopes, too. But I don't want to go back."

"Well, Alma, I don't want to go upstairs to that hot kitchen, either. But we need the money. So I want you to take the job. Try it out for a few weeks, at least."

"Then can I quit?"

Clara tucked her hair under the net. "We'll see," she said.

Six

On Saturday morning, Alma ate a breakfast of tea with toast and blueberry jam, brushed her teeth, put on her coat and slipped quietly out the back door, locking it behind her.

It was a sunny day and the air was chilly, carrying the heavy scent of seaweed, sand and salt, the sharp tang of autumn leaves. Alma walked quickly down Little Wharf Road. She didn't want to be late on the first official day of her first official job. Because it faced west, the front of the Chenoweth house, as Alma now thought of it, was in shadow. Since her first visit, the porch railing had been repaired and painted. The dormer stared down on the street like a Cyclops eye. Alma thought of Hansel and

Gretel finding the witch's house in the forest. She crossed the street and lifted the knocker.

Miss Olivia bade Alma good morning and let her in. Alma returned her greeting, noticing that, under the flower fragrance that seemed to envelope Miss Olivia like a cloud, was the faint whiff of perspiration.

The cardboard cartons had been cleared away from the hallway. The odour of fried bacon and coffee hung in the air, and Alma could see the breakfast dishes on the kitchen table. Miss Olivia showed Alma into the sitting room. Just as she had promised, there was a folder on the desk to the left of the green blotter and another folder to the right.

"Everything is ready, Alma," Miss Olivia said. "Call out if you need me. I'll just be in the kitchen."

"Yes, Miss Olivia."

Alma seated herself and opened the left file folder. Briefly, she savoured a wicked thought: if she made a poor job of copying this morning, Miss Lily might fire her, and Alma wouldn't have to return to this spooky house anymore. The folder contained three sheets of paper, each with typing on it. She took a leaf of the creamy writing paper from the pigeonhole and placed it on top of a lined page, picked up the pen, lifted the brass lid of the inkwell, dipped the pen nib into the black liquid and began to copy.

> *Dear Mr. O'Hare,*
>   *Allow me to express my gratitude for your assistance in putting my affairs in order prior to our removal to Charlotte's Bight. Though the circumstances leading to our decision were not at all happy, my daughter and I are resigned. . . .*

When she had finished the body of the letter, Alma wrote "Sincerely," followed by a comma, and left space for Miss Lily's name. She took an envelope from the pigeonhole and wrote out the address, a law firm in Rockport, Massachusetts. Then she put down the pen. She got up from the desk and stepped into the hall.

"Miss Olivia," she called out.

Olivia Chenoweth looked up from the kitchen table, which she was wiping down with a large rag.

"Um," Alma began.

"Yes, dear?"

"You didn't tell me the return address," Alma said. "To put on the envelope."

"You needn't include it," she said, rather abruptly.

"Oh," Alma replied, frowning. That's strange, she thought. At school we learned always to include the return address. It's a rule.

She went back to the desk. The second letter was to someone named Madeleine.

> *We have arrived and are set up in our new home, a modest but snug little spot by the harbour. Thank you again for your help. Should you wish to write to Olivia or me, you may send your letters to the usual address.*

The third was also short. It was addressed to a library in a place called Cambridge.

> *Dear Mrs. Gatwick,*
> *Thank you for your invitation to visit your library and speak with your patrons. I fear I must decline, however, because I have recently moved.*

There were two more letters. It was past ten when Alma slipped the last sheet into the folder to the right. She carefully cleaned the brass nib and placed the pen in its holder. Pushing back her chair, she got up just as Miss Olivia entered the room.

"Quite finished, Alma?"

"Yes, Miss Olivia."

"Excellent. Then you'll be on your way. See you next time."

When Alma got home, it was almost noon, and her mother was sitting at the kitchen table in slippers and bathrobe, a cup of tea before her and an open book propped against the teapot.

On the floor by the icebox was a large cloth bag. The week's laundry. Later, they would haul it to the old house by the park on Springbank Road, where Mrs. Squires took in laundry from the Liffey Pub and several restaurants. She kept three electric washing machines in her cellar, and on Saturday afternoons she rented one of them to Clara for a couple of hours.

Clara would grocery shop while Alma sat under the bare bulb that hung from the ceiling, reading, accompanied by the *slosh-slosh* of the washer. When the wind-up timer on the shelf gave off its piercing ring, she would run the clothes through the wringer, cranking the handle with both hands as the clothes slipped into the rinse tub.

Clara put down her book. "There's a drop of tea left."

"No, thanks, Mom."

"Well, sit down anyway and tell me all about this new family in the Stewart house."

"It's the Chenoweth house now," Alma said with authority.

"Is it, indeed, then? So what about the occupants of the Chenoweth house?"

Her mother loved gossip. Whatever she picked up from Alma would be passed on over drinks and dinner orders and tubs of dirty dishes in the kitchen of the Liffey Pub. Dutifully, Alma told all she knew.

"So you didn't see the old one today? The Miss Havisham woman?"

"Miss Lily. No. And Olivia Chenoweth smells. And she has a space between her two front teeth."

"So you've said. And what about these letters?"

Alma sat up straight in her chair. "Mom, I had to swear not to talk about them. They're private. Miss Olivia said I should think of myself as a pen that writes them but doesn't understand. Or something like that."

Clara stirred her cold tea. "I guess you're right. You wouldn't be much of a secretary if you blabbed, would you? Well, let's get dressed and get some work done."

"I am dressed," Alma said.

"So you are. Then while I don my finest apparel, you can do up the dishes."

CHAPTER

Seven

One Monday after school Alma headed for the library, carrying her school bag. The trees around the square had turned blazing red and orange, and a chilly rain pattered on the broad leaves, knocking some of them to the soggy grass.

To Alma, the large double door of panelled oak, shiny with varnish, adorned with long tubular brass handles darkened by many hands, was like the portal to a castle. She stepped inside and shook the rain from her coat before hanging it alongside six or seven others on the rack by the door, eyes averted from the stairs to the darkened basement, where, according to Robbie Thornton, the ghost of a dead janitor lurked.

"Of course he's dead," Alma had sneered when Robbie told her the story of how the janitor had hanged himself from the steam pipe. "He couldn't be a ghost otherwise, could he?"

Robbie seemed to think every building in Charlotte's Bight harboured a haunt somewhere in its dark corners. Alma was certain—almost— that he had made up the tale about the janitor. He told the stories just to get attention, she thought. Still, she kept her eyes fixed ahead as she mounted the three steps to the reading room and circulation desk.

There were a few people in the reading room, standing among the stacks or perusing newspapers at one of the broad tables in the centre. Alma caught sight of Louise Arsenault in the fiction section, with Polly Switzer and Samantha Keith, two of her most loyal followers. Alma pointedly ignored them and listened to the quiet, punctuated by the *click, click* of the old clock, with its hexagonal face and Gothic numerals, on the wall above the circulation desk. At the far end of the room, she saw her mother pushing a book cart among the stacks, pausing to replace a book, then moving on. When Clara looked up, Alma waved.

Alma's first stop was the card catalogue. Miss McAllister had given the class an arts assignment that morning. The students were to choose an author and write a one-page biography by Friday.

She opened the R–S drawer of the author file and quickly found the card for Hawkins, RR. The seven books Alma was familiar with were listed, the trilogy and the series of four, but no others. It seemed that the owner of the Turnaround had been right, Alma thought with disappointment, for she had continued to nourish the hope that she would find other books by her favourite author. The card catalogue's "Subject" section listed no biography of RR Hawkins.

Miss McGregor, the head librarian, wasn't present that day. Alma liked her because she knew everything and was very eager to share her knowledge, sometimes too anxious. Alma went to the reference section, which was the kingdom of Mr. Winters, a skinny young man with dark, oily hair combed straight back. He always wore a white shirt and tie and his leather shoes squeaked. He looked up from a list he was making when Alma stood before his desk and said, "Ahem."

"How may I help you?" he asked without enthusiasm.

"I have to write a biography of my favourite author. For school. But I can't find anything about him."

Mr. Winters put down his pen and laced his fingers together as if about to deliver a speech. "In whom are you interested?"

"RR Hawkins."

"Afraid I don't know him. You've tried the catalogue?"

"Yes."

"The encyclopedias? *Who's Who*?"

"No."

Mr. Winters pointed to the stack nearest him. "Over there," he said.

"Thank you."

Alma's mother was slipping the P volume of an encyclopedia into its proper place when Alma turned to the shelves.

"Hello, dear," Clara said.

"Hi, Mom."

Her mother had come to the library directly from her noon shift at the Liffey. Her clothes smelled of cigarette smoke and cooking oil.

"*Shhhhhhh!*" Mr. Winters admonished them.

Clara dropped her voice to a whisper. "I'll shush you, Mr. High-and-mighty," she hissed.

Alma giggled. Clara and Mr. Winters were always at odds. "He's not exactly the type to get down on the floor and play with the dog, is he?" Clara had once said of him. He acted as if he was Clara's boss, but he wasn't. Miss McGregor was.

"What are you after today?" Clara asked.

Alma told her about the project as she pulled down the H volumes of the three sets of encyclopedias and the *Who's Who*.

"Well, that should be a stroll in the park for you," Clara said. "I've got to keep going." She pushed the book cart down the row, passing Louise and her friends, who had come to the reference section.

Polly wrinkled her nose. "I smell french fries," she said in a stage whisper.

"Suddenly I'm in the mood for fish and chips," Samantha said with a giggle, just loud enough for Alma to hear.

The three girls moved toward the check-out desk.

Bet you wouldn't think it was funny if I pushed the bunch of you down the basement stairs, Alma thought, slapping one volume against another and earning a scowl from Mr. Winters. She took the heavy books to one of the tables and began her search. A few minutes later, she returned the volumes to their places, even though it was against the rules to reshelve books. But if she left them on the table her mother would have to replace them.

Back in front of Mr. Winters's desk, she said, "Ahem."

"Any luck?" Mr. Winters asked.

"No. Is there anything else I can try?"

"There are the vertical files, I suppose." Mr. Winters rose slowly from his chair and went through a door behind him. He came back a few minutes later with a large folder in his hands.

"You're in luck," he said, handing the file to Alma. "Reference only, by the way," he added. "You can't take it out of the library and you'll have to use it right there." He pointed to the table nearest his desk. "Do not change the order of the contents or write on them or damage them in any way."

"Yes, *sir*," Alma said mockingly.

Mr. Winters gave her a cold look. "The library closes in half an hour."

Alma carried the file to the table and sat down. She took a writing tablet and pencil from her school bag, then pulled on the black ribbon that held the musty folder closed. There wasn't much inside—some newspaper clippings, a copy of a magazine article—Alma could tell from the glossy pages—and book reviews. She began to read and to make notes.

RR Hawkins, she discovered, had been born in New York City, the only child of a wealthy businessman, James Earl Hawkins. RR's mother wasn't named. The RR stood for Rachel Rebecca.

Alma had always assumed that the person who had created Centreworld and Alterworld, who had drawn the maps and invented the creatures who lived in those places and the languages they spoke, was a man.

"Female!!!" Alma wrote on her pad. "Rachel Rebecca Hawkins."

For some reason, her discovery made her glad. She read on. RR Hawkins had moved with her parents to London, England, when she was twelve. Later, she went to Cambridge University and took her degree in ancient and medieval history. Alma got up and walked to the wooden stand where the big Webster's Dictionary rested, to look up "medieval." "Of, or imitating the Middle Ages," she read, sighing as she crossed to the stacks and took down the M volume of an encyclopedia. "The period between A.D. 400 and A.D. 1500," she read under "Middle Ages."

She returned to her chair to find her mother picking up books left there by other patrons and arranging them in order on the book cart.

"Might as well walk home together," Clara said.

"Sure, Mom."

"How's the research going?"

"Great. I discovered RR Hawkins was a woman."

"Did you, now?"

"At least, I think she's a 'was.' Maybe she's an 'is.' I haven't found out yet. I'll have to come back tomorrow. I can't take the file home."

"No, it's Reference," Clara said, moving away. "We wouldn't want to upset his highness," she whispered, pointing toward Mr. Winters's desk with her chin.

Alma laughed and got back to work. She read a book review of RR's first novel, *Circle of Doom*. The reviewer heaped compliments on the book, called RR a "major new talent" and predicted the novel, "a stunner," would win prizes. *Circle of Doom* was quickly published in many languages. RR became a very wealthy young—

"The library is closing." Mr. Winters stood behind his desk.

Alma carefully aligned the documents and placed them in the file. She retied the ribbon, giving it a sharp tug, and carried the folder to Mr. Winters.

"Clara, if you would," he said, passing the file to Alma's mother, who was parking the book cart against the wall.

She took the folder and walked through the door behind Mr. Winters's desk. When she came back out buttoning her raincoat, she had a shopping bag on her arm.

"Let's go," she said to Alma. "I'm famished."

Darkness had fallen and the rain had stopped. Alma and her mother strolled the short distance to the alley, which was pocked with puddles reflecting the light from nearby windows. Once home, they hung up their coats in the alcove and Alma went to the hot plate to put on the kettle.

Clara opened her shopping bag and removed the folder on RR Hawkins. She dropped it onto the kitchen table, smiling.

"Mom!" Alma exclaimed.

"Do you think you can finish your reading tonight while I'm at work?" Clara asked.

"Sure, but won't Mr. Win—?"

"What he doesn't know won't hurt him," Clara said.

With supper done, the dishes washed and put away, the kitchen floor swept and the tea things laid out for Clara's return late that night, Alma sat at the table and opened the file again.

Circle of Doom had been followed two years later by *The Gathering Darkness,* and, two years after that, *The Rising* completed the trilogy, making RR Hawkins a very famous and wealthy woman. But things in her personal life, the little that Alma could piece together from the book reviews, weren't going well. RR Hawkins moved away from London, on her own, and then dropped out of sight. She became a recluse. Someone wrote an article saying she had joined a convent; another referred to a failed marriage; someone else claimed she had died, a bit of hearsay contradicted when the first novel in the Alterworld series, *Into the Shadows,* came out.

Alma was angry when she read a so-called news report that the Alterworld books had been written by someone else, under RR Hawkins's name.

"That's stupid," Alma muttered, making notes. "You can tell she wrote all the Alterworld books."

By the time she reached the last facts, Alma had two pages of neatly written information in point form. I didn't find out much, she mused, but I can complete my report. Maybe I'll ask Miss McGregor if she knows where I can get more information. At the end of it all, Alma's favourite author was as much a mystery as ever. The final article in the file confirmed Alma's worst fear.

INTERNATIONALLY RENOWNED AUTHOR PUTS DOWN PEN

A spokesman for Seabord Press, publisher of all seven internationally renowned novels by fantasy fiction phenomenon RR Hawkins, announced today the reclusive writer has vowed never to write another book.

Hawkins, who wrote her seven smash hits over a period of some fifteen years, has remained in seclusion for virtually all of her career.

"Her readers don't know where she lives or what she looks like. Nothing about her personal life is known to the public. That's the way she has wanted it and we have honoured her wishes," said Seabord's Editor in Chief, Stephen Knowles. "Now, she has told us her writing career is at an end. With regret, we must accept her decision."

The object of much speculation and rumour over the years, Hawkins has, according to many in the publishing world, taken her wish for privacy to the point of eccentricity.

Asked what RR Hawkins's plans for the future might be, Knowles said, "Your guess is as good as mine."

CHAPTER

Eight

On Tuesday, Alma made her way to the Chenoweth house after school. She was let in by Miss Olivia and went directly to her place at the desk. As darkness crept up the face of the buildings opposite the big window—daylight faded early at that time of year—Alma copied the three letters in the folder.

"Dear Mr. Vranckx, I am so glad you enjoyed the book," the first letter began, "and that you took the time to write." More pleasantries followed, then "Sincerely." Alma took an envelope and wrote Mr. Vranckx's name and address on the front, surprised to see the destination was Belgium.

The next letter was to a Mr. Wharton. "Dear

Sir," Alma copied carefully, "I am most grateful for your invitation to address your conference. Unfortunately, I must decline, as I am not available on the dates indicated." This letter ended, "Regretfully," and the address was Montreal.

There was one more letter. "Dear Margaret Stanhope, I am in receipt of your second letter requesting an interview and must once again disappoint you." More expressions of regret followed, and, Alma thought, a slight impatience between the lines, as if Miss Lily was put out with Margaret Stanhope.

Alma had developed the ability to copy and at the same time allow her mind to wander, and when her thoughts strayed, they usually went toward one of her own stories. Today, she recalled Superdumb, a hero she had written about two years before. He was blond and handsome. He wore a light blue outfit with a crimson cape that swirled like the wind when he moved. Superdumb was tall and strong and he could fly. He had a kind heart and hated to see people, especially children, sad or suffering. But he wasn't very smart. He got confused easily. So when he was little the local bully nicknamed him Superdumb.

Superdumb soared around the town and helped people. He pushed cars out of snowdrifts, brought frightened cats down from trees, found lost dogs and budgies. He broke up fights in the schoolyard and turned thieves in to the police. Alma liked him. He was dumb, but had a heart of gold.

"Superdumb went flying down the park" was the first line she wrote at her desk in the third row. Her teacher that year, Mr. Drake, stopped beside her.

"You can't say 'flying down the park,' Alma," he told her. "You can say 'flying through' or 'flying over the park.'"

"But we say 'driving down the road,'" Alma replied. "And 'running down to the harbour.'"

A frown creased Mr. Drake's long face just above his eyes. "And you mustn't call someone Dumb. It's rude."

"But Superdumb doesn't mind," Alma said. "He—"

"It won't do, Alma," her teacher said sternly. "Begin again."

So Alma scratched out the first line and wrote, "Once there was a squirrel named Bob." Mr. Drake nodded wisely and moved on. When she got home that day, Alma completed

her Superdumb story and put it in a cardboard
box where she kept all the tales she had written.

"Alma, could you do me a favour?"

Miss Olivia's words snatched Alma back to the
present. She turned to see the plump woman
pulling on her coat, her glass beads—yellow
today—rattling. "I've got to dash out for a few
minutes for Miss Lily's medicine. If you hear her
bell, just go on in to her room. All right?"

"Er, yes," Alma replied. I'd rather not, she
didn't say.

The door closed, and Alma saw Miss Olivia
hurry down the walk and turn up the street.
Alma had one more letter to copy. When she
was halfway through, she heard the tinkle of a
bell. She got up, passed the kitchen and
knocked on Miss Lily's door.

"Come in, Alma," she heard.

Miss Lily's room had changed. On the
shelves sat row upon row of books, most of
them bound in cloth or leather. A typewriter,
ungainly and black, sat on one of the desks
beside a stack of paper, and a telephone, also
black, had been installed.

Miss Lily was replacing the bell on the table
beside her when Alma entered. She wore the
same shawl over a navy blue dress that gave no

colour to her pale features. Old-fashioned leather shoes, the kind that laced up, peeped out from under the hem. A cigarette burned in the ivory holder between her fingers.

"How are you, dear?"

"I'm fine, Miss Lily," Alma replied, still not comfortable with the idea of addressing this fearsome-looking elderly woman, with her thick eyebrows and axe-blade nose, as Miss. "How are you?"

"I'm old and arthritic and therefore grumpy, I suppose," she said, with a hint of a smile at the turned-down corners of her mouth. "I've dropped my cigarette lighter. It's there, under Olivia's desk."

Alma got down on her hands and knees and peered into the dark knee-well of the desk. She reached in and retrieved the lighter, an ornate, heavy rendition of an urn.

"Put it on the table, beside my cigarettes," Miss Lily directed. "And sit down."

Alma did as she was told.

"Now, I want you to tell me about yourself, your family, everything," Miss Lily said. "Begin."

Alma faltered at first, unsure where to start. She told Miss Lily where she lived and went to school, described her mother's two jobs, at the library and the pub, and confided that Clara was hoping for a promotion to waitress.

"A promotion to waitress," Miss Lily said in her deep voice as her eyebrows rose. "Go on. You haven't mentioned your father. Is he dead?"

Alma hated that word; she never said it or thought it. She merely nodded.

"Do you have many friends?"

"Not very many," Alma replied, thinking "almost none" would be more accurate. "Mom doesn't like me to bring girls to our house—apartment. She says she's too busy." But I know the real reason, Alma didn't say. She's ashamed. She doesn't want people to see where we live, or they'd gossip. Living in an apartment under a pub, how awful, they'd say.

"Well, what do you do with your time?" Miss Lily asked impatiently, as if Alma wasn't living up to her expectations. "Do you listen to the radio?"

"No, we don't have one. I like to read. And write stories. I want to be an author when I grow up."

"Do you, indeed? And who is your favourite?"

"That's easy," Alma replied. "RR Hawkins."

"Indeed," Miss Lily repeated.

Alma sat silently, unsure of what to say next.

"At any rate," Miss Lily finally said, "your handwriting is satisfactory, and your work, too."

"Thank you," Alma said.

"You are interested in calligraphy, are you not?" Miss Lily said, making the question sound like an accusation. She screwed the end of a cigarette into the ivory holder and lit it with the urn-lighter, manipulating the objects awkwardly, as if her fingers wouldn't bend properly.

"Yes."

"Are you aware, Alma," Miss Lily said, taking a deep puff on the cigarette, "that there was a time—before the invention of the printing press and movable type—when all books were copied by hand, and calligraphy was more than an art form but also a highly desirable and necessary skill? In monasteries all over Europe, thousands of monks kept books alive by copying them and storing them in libraries. Some of the manuscripts were illustrated with coloured inks. Quite beautiful. You've never heard of the *Book of Kells*, I don't suppose? It was written around the year 800, in insular majuscule."

"No, Miss Lily." Or monasteries, or insular whatever, or something-or-other type, Alma didn't say. She had heard of monks, but didn't know what monks did or where they lived.

"Go to the bookshelf. Second row from the top, right side."

Alma followed her directions.

"The thin, tall book. Bring it down."

Standing on her tiptoes, Alma slid a leather-bound book from the shelf and handed it to Miss Lily.

"No, Alma. It's for you. To borrow. Take a look inside."

Alma opened the cover and flipped a few gilt-edged pages. The paper was glossy. The book showed different kinds of writing—Italic, Carolingian, uncial, Roman.

"When you leave today, tell Olivia to give you a spare pen and a few nibs. Do you have ink at home?"

"No."

Miss Lily looked at her as if she had just said, We have no food. "Take a bottle with you."

"Yes, Miss Lily."

"Good. Now you may go back to your work."

Alma took the book to the sitting room. By the time Miss Olivia returned, she had finished her letter copying and was looking through the calligraphy book. Alma told her about the pen, nibs and ink. Miss Olivia's eyebrows rose, but she gave the items to Alma, who carried them home in her school bag like prizes won at a county fair.

CHAPTER

Nine

At the kitchen table, with a checkerboard wedged upside down between her lap and the table, and the calligraphy book propped open before her, Alma practised her "hand." She had examined the calligraphic styles described in Miss Lily's book and decided she liked Carolingian and half-uncials the best. Gothic was too dark and stiff and aggressive, Italic was too showy, Roman too blockish. The problem was, her pen nib was pointed and the book said you should have a squared nib so you could make thick lines with downstrokes and thin lines with upstrokes.

She wrote slowly and precisely, learning the strokes required to form each letter. It was much more fun than penmanship at school on Tuesdays and Thursdays.

A thump on the inside door told her that her mother was home for supper.

"Mom, can I get a calligraphy pen?" Alma asked.

"For the love of heaven, Alma, let me get my foot in the door before you start in," Clara said. "Why isn't the table set?"

Alma screwed the cap on the ink bottle, cleaned her pen with a tissue, closed the book and carried everything away into her room. Once back in the kitchen, she took down two plates from the cupboard and began to set the table around the grease-stained package in the middle.

"Fish and chips?" Alma said unnecessarily, since the odour of battered fish and oily french fries had already filled the tiny kitchen.

"I was able to get my hands on some halibut this time," Clara said from the sink where she was washing her hands. Seated, with their luke-warm food before them, Clara asked, "Now, what's all this about a pen?"

As she halved each french fry, Alma explained the book Miss Lily had lent her and the pen and ink. "I think she used to be a librarian," she added, "like Miss McGregor. She loves books, and she knows a lot about them."

"You're quite the pals now, are you?" Clara said.

"I don't think so, Mom. She still scares me. She practically *made* me borrow this book. But I'm glad she did."

"And why weren't you writing your report when I came home?"

"I'm going to finish it tonight. It's almost done. I still have to colour the cover page. And you're changing the subject."

"The subject?" Clara asked innocently, popping a wilted french fry into her mouth.

"The pen, Mom."

"Oh, the pen. A calligraphy pen, no less."

"With a square nib."

"We'll see."

"You always say that."

"True. But we'll see."

With the kitchen seen to and her mother back to work, Alma completed her report on RR Hawkins, squeezing crayon bits between thumb and forefinger as she coloured the map of Otherworld she had drawn on her cover page.

I wonder why RR Hawkins quit writing, Alma thought. Maybe she died. No, that can't be. The newspaper story said she just stopped. Alma looked at her report. She had two pages filled with writing, but still there were more questions than answers. What, after all, did she know about Hawkins? Everything was there; Hawkins was born, went to London, England, at twelve years of age, got her university degree, left home—and disappeared.

So, Alma decided as she gathered up her crayon bits, something happened when RR Hawkins was in her early twenties, something that made her flee human contact. Maybe she came down with a horrible, disfiguring skin disease that ravaged her face and drove her into hiding. Maybe she had become engaged to a handsome young man whom she loved more than life itself, but he was killed in a war (dying a heroic death) and she vowed to remain single and reclusive forever. Maybe she decided to travel the world and was captured by a band of vagabonds who—No, Alma checked herself, that's silly. Still, you never knew.

Whatever it was hadn't deterred RR Hawkins from writing stories. She continued to publish. Something made her stop eventually, though, Alma thought as she left her report on the kitchen table beside Clara's teacup. Maybe Miss McGregor will have some ideas.

When Alma got up the next morning, Clara was already in the kitchen, humming and flipping pancakes in the iron skillet, her thick braid swinging back and forth across her back as she worked. Alma washed and dressed and combed her hair, then sat down at the table. The stack of pancakes had been topped with a big square of yellow butter. Alma poured maple syrup on the pancakes, licking her lips in anticipation. When her mother had sat down, Alma dug in.

"Bet I know the answer," Clara said, squinting and arching her brows mysteriously.

Alma couldn't speak for a moment. Her mouth was full. "Answer?"

"I read your report. Your author left home alone, right? And that would have been almost, what, fifty years ago."

"Yes."

"So, here's my guess. She took up with a young man her family didn't approve of—they were very rich and likely snobbish along with it. They forced her to break it off with him, or bribed him to go away. She was bitter and left her family. Bitter at him, too, I wouldn't be surprised. What do you think?" Clara smiled mischievously.

Alma chewed slowly on the last bite of sweet, buttery pancake. "I wonder if I should write that in the report," she teased.

"No, I wouldn't. For one thing, you don't know it to be true. It's just a story spun by your mother. Second, you wouldn't want to ruffle Miss McAllister's feathers with talk of illicit goings on with men below one's station."

"I wonder if Miss McAllister has a boyfriend," Alma mused. Then a thought struck her. "Do you think I'll ever have one?"

"What, a beautiful, intelligent child like yourself? It's only a matter of time."

Alma noticed that the playful look had left her mother's face. Bet I know what you're thinking, she didn't say. Bet you're lonely sometimes.

Although she had finished her report and handed it in to Miss McAllister, who praised the colourful title page with its Carolingian lettering, Alma went to the library for one more try.

Whenever she saw Miss McGregor, Alma thought briefly—and, she hoped, not unkindly—

of the blue herons that waded in the shallows of the Springbank River. The librarian had a long neck and legs like stilts. Her feet stuck out to the sides, her hands were big and bony. Behind her wire-rim spectacles, Miss McGregor's complexion was florid, her broad, high forehead shiny, her black hair pulled back severely in a tight bun.

A person has to be careful when talking to Miss McGregor, Alma reminded herself as she approached the counter behind which the head librarian sat over her desk. If you asked Miss McGregor, "Do you have any books on such-and-such?" she would tow you through the stacks like a barge, loading your arms with books and chattering away about each volume as she plopped it on the pile. It helped if you could make your question as exact as possible.

"Hello, Alma," Miss McGregor said from her chair.

They exchanged pleasantries for a few minutes, then Alma got to the point. "I'm trying to find out as much as I can about RR Hawkins," she began, "and—"

"Wonderful writer!" Miss McGregor exclaimed as she jumped to her feet like a meadowlark taking flight. "Wonderful. Come on, I'll—"

"No, wait!" Alma exclaimed, bringing the librarian to a halt. "Um, I've looked at everything here, and—"

"The encyclopedias?" Miss McGregor queried, somewhat crestfallen. "The *Who's Who*?"

"Yes," Alma replied.

Miss McGregor raised her finger as if to make a point. "Ah, but we've a vertical file on RR Hawkins. Let me—"

"Read it," Alma cut in, feeling almost guilty.

"Hmm," Miss McGregor said to herself, returning to her chair and folding her legs under her desk.

"I was just wondering if you know of anywhere else I could look," Alma said.

Miss McGregor pointed to a chair beside her desk. "Sit down, dear."

Alma slid into the wooden chair.

"There's one more thing we can try," Miss McGregor said. "I don't think there are any biographies of RR Hawkins, but I'll make enquiries, just to be sure. And we'll try an inter-library loan. One of the larger libraries may have something. We try our best here, but we're a small operation compared to some."

"Thank you, Miss McGregor."

"She'd be proud, you know," the head librarian said, nodding her head. "RR Hawkins would. If she knew that you loved her books so much."

CHAPTER

Ten

The first storm of the season roared out of the northeast, driving snow before it like a flock of manic sheep. Alma walked to school with icy flakes pelting her face and at the end of the day slogged through more than a foot of snow, the bitter wind at her back, coating her with white as she pushed down Little Wharf Road to the Chenoweth house.

After her duties in the cosy sitting room had been performed, Alma headed home in the dark. The alley behind the Liffey was rutted and churned by delivery trucks, and the door to the apartment wouldn't open until she cleared away the snow with a broom her mother had left leaning against the building.

There was a note on the table. "Come meet me at the library," it said. Alma sighed, put her coat and hat, mitts and boots back on, locked up and headed for the library. She arrived just as her mother came out the big oak doors, wrapping her scarf around her neck.

"Come on," she said. "We're eating at a restaurant tonight!"

A restaurant! Alma couldn't remember the last time she'd been in one. A waste of money, Clara always said. What had changed her mind?

"What's your fancy, young Miss?" Clara asked.

"Anything but fish and potatoes."

Clara laughed. "Fair enough."

A short while later they were seated in a booth at the Fireside Café, a silly name, Alma thought, since the restaurant had no fireplace. The window looking onto the street was coated in steam, the blue-and-white checkered table-cloth fresh and crisp. The restaurant was, despite the weather, crowded, and the odour of damp clothes competed with the fragrance of grilled steak and onions, the Fireside's famous vegetable soup, and coffee.

Alma had a tall cola with ice and a long straw in front of her. Clara sipped a cup of steaming coffee.

They had ordered spaghetti with meatballs, and Alma knew something very important was happening when Clara asked the waitress to put aside two pieces of apple pie for their dessert. Alma looked around as they waited for their food.

"Well," Clara began, pulling Alma's attention back to the table, "you're probably wondering what's going on."

Alma nodded, slurping the last bit of cola up the straw.

"You're now looking at Liffey's new waitress!" her mother said, smiling. "That means a small raise, more hours, and tips!"

"That's great, Mom," Alma said.

"And it means I could buy you this," Clara added, placing a small box before Alma. "It's a bit early for Christmas, so let's call it an un-birthday present."

"What is it?" Alma asked, though she could guess from the shape of the box.

"Open it and see."

Alma removed the coloured paper carefully so it could be taken home and reused. Inside was a white box with red trim. Alma opened it.

The pen was black, with a brass clip on the cap and a brass circle near the base of the barrel.

Alma pulled off the cap. The nib had a square tip. "Waterman" was etched into the gold-coloured nib in graceful flowing letters.

"A calligraphy pen! It's beautiful," Alma said, looking up. "Can I keep it?"

"Of course, ninny."

"Honest and true?"

"Honest and true." Clara smiled. "You can use it to write your stories."

"Thanks, Mom." The cap went *click* when Alma replaced it. "I'm going to write a story in Carolingian hand first. It's more than a thousand years old. Then I'll write one in half-uncials. That's the hand used in Ireland from 600 to 800. It's not as old, but it's prettier."

The waitress arrived and placed plates of steaming spaghetti on the table.

"Cheers," Clara said.

"Cheers," said Alma, clinking her water glass against her mother's.

When Alma came home from school Friday she found a bulging file on the kitchen table, an accordion-sided container with a string on the flap wound around a stiff paper button. "RR Hawkins" had been written on the edge of the file with a fountain pen above a label that said "Inter-library Loan." A note from Clara said Miss McGregor had sent it home with her. Alma could keep the file for a day or two, but it must be returned Monday at the latest.

Alma shucked off her coat and hung it up. She took the file to her room, sat on the couch and unwound the string. She lifted the papers out and put the folder aside. Alma slid to the floor and, using the couch as a desktop, began to go through the material, all the while hoping against hope that there would be more books by RR Hawkins. There were newspaper stories, magazine articles, book reviews, just as the other file had contained, but more—not much more, but some. Alma got out her new calligraphy pen and began to make notes.

After RR Hawkins disappeared, she moved to New York and attempted to remain unnoticed, but interest in her as a writer was high and she was found out. She had a baby, a girl, letting it be known that her husband was still in England. "Maybe Mom was right!" Alma noted in brackets. The press eventually dug up the fact that there was no husband. There was a scandal that drove RR Hawkins into hiding again.

She was discovered, a few years later, by a fan, in a Boston department store. The press pounced on her again. But this time she apparently decided not to run. She had bought a large house in one of the better neighbourhoods and refused all requests for interviews and public appearances. It was almost, Alma thought as she read, as if the more people wanted RR Hawkins to be public, the deeper they drove her into seclusion.

RR Hawkins continued to publish. Her daughter grew up, went to college, married a composer and moved away; Alma couldn't find out where. The husband died young. Overcome by grief, RR Hawkins's daughter returned home to her mother. She never remarried. She seemed to desire seclusion as much as her mother.

There was one last item in the file. On a scrap of yellowed newsprint was a photo of two women emerging from the door of an imposing, two-storey house. One was considerably taller than the other. Their faces were shadowed by the overhanging verandah. The caption under the photo said, "Seen at their house on **Kavanagh Street in Boston are the author RR Hawkins and her daughter, Olivia.**"

Eleven

*C*ould it be? Alma wondered. She did a quick calculation in her head. Yes, Miss Lily was about the right age. Had she and Miss Olivia moved to Charlotte's Bight from Boston? Were they on the run, attempting to find an out-of-the-way place to live a private life? No. Impossible. The question and answer buzzed round in her head like pesky mosquitoes. Unable to put the issue out of her mind, she grabbed a sheet of paper and drew a line down the centre. At the top of the column on the left she wrote "Could be" and, so excited that she didn't bother to form her letters properly, she put "Not possible" above the right-hand column, adding an exclamation mark for good measure.

What were the clues? she asked herself.

1. "Miss Lily is tall, like the woman in the photo," Alma noted in the left column. On the right side she wrote, "Lots of women are tall!"

2. "Miss Lily likes books." "Lots of people like books, including me, and Mom, even Miss McAllister. And Miss McGregor."

3. "The letters I copy for Miss Lily sometimes refuse interviews and invitations to talk to audiences, the kind of requests made of famous people." Alma could think of nothing to put down in the right-hand column.

4. "Miss Lily's letters have no return address, as if she doesn't want people to know where the letters come from." "That's silly," Alma scribbled on the right side of the line. How could she *get* the letters she was answering if the sender didn't know where she lived? Unless the letters came to her indirectly. Through her publisher, maybe. Alma penned a question mark between the columns.

5. "It's *Miss* Lily, not Mrs. Somebody." As if the old woman in the dark study who reminded Alma of Miss Havisham had never married.

6. "Miss Lily has a daughter named Olivia *Chenoweth*." Alma had always thought Chenoweth was the surname of both women.

But if Olivia had married and her husband had died, she'd have a different surname, her husband's.

7. So, they could be Olivia Chenoweth and Lily Hawkins. On the right, Alma reluctantly scribbled, "Lily doesn't begin with an R!!!"

8. But, "Could Miss RR Hawkins have another name? A nickname or a family name?" Alma couldn't imagine Miss Lily accepting a nickname.

Alma had been thinking so hard, her head hurt. Time and time again she told herself her imagination was running wild. To think a world-famous writer would come to live in an old wooden house in an out-of-the-way place like Charlotte's Bight! Alma decided she was being a dunce. She wanted RR Hawkins to be close by, so her mind was making things up. She had always put RR Hawkins on the list of authors she would love to talk to, so she was trying to make it come true.

Still, she insisted, it *could* be.

Alma decided to find out, once and for all.

She would have to think like a detective. She must, when at Miss Lily's house, keep her eyes open. Observe, like Sherlock Holmes. But she had to wait. She couldn't just march over to the Chenoweth house, push open the big wooden door and snoop through the place with a giant magnifying glass. It would be three days before she had the opportunity to put her plan into action.

Even then, how *could* she find the answer to the mystery? Alma repeatedly asked herself over the next few days. She could simply ask Miss Lily, but that seemed rude, especially if Alma was right. It would mean that all Miss Lily's efforts to keep her identity secret had failed. Alma didn't want to be the one to let the secret out, the way Pandora had released the evils from her box.

The following Tuesday afternoon as Alma was ambling home from school, enjoying the sunshine, she caught sight of Russell Stearns, walking jauntily along the sidewalk on Grafton Street, his black postman's bag fat with letters, his blue uniform rumpled, his ruddy cheeks puffed up as he whistled tunelessly.

"Afternoon, Alma," he said as he passed.

"Hi, Russell," Alma replied. Then, to herself she whispered, "Of course! Why didn't I think of it before? It's perfect!"

She started to run.

⟨≈⟩

"Dear RR Hawkins," she began, barely able to contain her excitement as she wrote, in pencil, with an ugly backward slant to disguise her own hand.

Alma was sitting on the rug in her room, a sheet of plain writing paper in front of her. She had already addressed the envelope to RR Hawkins, c/o Seabord Publishing Company, New York City. Her plan was simple. If Alma's suspicions were correct and the woman she worked for was the famous author, the letter would come right back to Charlotte's Bight and Alma herself would copy the reply!

Alma struggled to hold herself back. She was tempted to put everything she wanted to say to RR Hawkins in the letter, but, she reminded herself, she might be wrong about Miss Lily. Best to go slowly, she told herself. So she wrote, "I have admired your books for a long time and I wanted to know if you have written anything since you finished the Alterworld Series." Alma left a space, then wrote, "Yours sincerely." She wrote the *A* in her name and then caught herself.

"Stupid!" she muttered, vigorously erasing the error. Then she wrote "Hattie Scrivener," because she had always liked the name Hattie (she had even tried to change her name to Hattie but her mother wouldn't let her), and a scrivener was a writer and Alma wanted to be a writer someday.

Then Alma thought of another problem. When she mailed the letter it would go to the post office in Charlotte's Bight, where the stamp would be cancelled before the letter was sent on to New York. The cancellation imprint would show the name of the town and the date. So Miss Olivia and Miss Lily would know where the letter originated.

"Oh, well," Alma concluded, "there's nothing I can do about that."

Another thought struck her: Miss Lily's letters to her fans *must* go back to her publisher to be mailed from there, otherwise every letter she sent would show that it was mailed in Charlotte's Bight! And in such a small place, she would be easy to find! That was why none of the envelopes Alma wrote out had return addresses!

She smiled to herself, pleased with her Holmesian powers of deduction and logic, as she sealed the letter to her favourite author inside its envelope. She placed the stamp exactly, in line with the top and right edge of the envelope. She put on her coat and went out to post the letter. Before she dropped it in the mailbox she crossed her fingers.

"Here's hoping," she said.

Twelve

While Alma waited impatiently to find out if her "Hattie Scrivener ploy," as she called it, was successful, she worked on her story. Miss McAllister had assigned a short story, to be completed before school broke for the summer holidays, and there was a prize for the best one. Alma wanted to win the prize.

"SAM-U-ELLLL!"
Uh-oh, Sammy thought.

Before long, she had completed chapter 1, where Sammy goes to the library and discovers a secret door.

⌒

As the days passed, Alma's excitement each time she entered Miss Lily's house diminished, until she went a whole day without once thinking about her clever trick to solve the RR Hawkins mystery. Alma began to fear that, as happened so often, she had let her imagination capture her and carry her off. Perhaps, after all, Miss Lily was just a slightly eccentric and more than slightly scary old lady living in Charlotte's Bight with her slightly eccentric daughter whose name happened to be Olivia.

Alma's home underwent changes. With her increased salary and longer hours, Clara was able to purchase bright, colourful material to make a tablecloth and curtains for the kitchen. She bought an almost complete set of dishes at a garage sale. "No more cracked teacups in *this* house," she told Alma on the day she brought home the cardboard carton full of dusty dishes with a cornflower pattern around the rims. There was a new doormat with "Welcome" printed on it, and a boot tray, and for Alma and her mother, new galoshes that didn't leak.

After the lending of the calligraphy book, the pen and ink, Alma had softened toward her employer, but was still a little shaken each time she was summoned to the room with the fireplace. One afternoon, when the weak winter light washed the sitting room where Alma worked, Miss Olivia told Alma, "When you're through today, Miss Lily would like to see you, dear."

Miss Lily was at her usual place, in the chair by the fire, a large book open on her lap, with a lit cigarette in the ivory holder. Alma was conscious of a tingling sensation in her stomach as she thought of the elaborate trick she was playing on her employer. Miss Lily put the cigarette holder in her mouth and closed the book, placing it on the table on top of two others. Alma read the titles on the spines. *Chess Problems from Ancient Persia. Philodor's Conundrum and Other Chess Challenges.* It was then that Alma noticed the chess set on the desk nearest the fire, elaborately carved pieces at rest on the board, as if waiting for something to happen.

"Hello, Miss Lily," she said when Miss Olivia closed the door behind her.

"How is your calligraphy coming along?" Miss Lily asked, her throaty voice intimidating Alma as it usually did.

"Fine, I think."

"Well, is it or isn't it?"

"Yes."

"Are you enjoying it?"

"I . . . I love it!" Alma gushed, in spite of herself. "My mother bought me a pen."

"I'm a little disappointed that you haven't shown any of your work to me," Miss Lily said, her stony voice a bit less stony, Alma thought. Or perhaps it was Miss Lily's habit of speaking as she exhaled a cloud of cigarette smoke.

"Oh, um, I could. If you wish."

"Bring some with you next time you come," Miss Lily commanded.

"Yes, Miss Lily."

"In the meantime, you say you like books by this Hawkins person."

"Yes! She's my favourite."

"Well, be that as it may, you may like that book there," she said, pointing to the bookshelf, "second shelf from the bottom, third section."

In a moment, Alma found it. *The Secret Orchard.*

"I've read it," Alma said.

"Fourth shelf from the top, fourth section. Clive Loomis."

"The *Rianna Chronicles* books? I've read them all," Alma said, a little worried she might be disappointing Miss Lily, who was clearly trying to be kind. "Three times," she added without knowing why.

"Hmm." The old woman's brow creased, but the thin lips seemed to fight off a smile. "*The Elvenland Trilogy*?" she asked.

"I beg your pardon?" Alma said.

"So, finally a book that has escaped your clutches. Geoffrey Reese. Top shelf, sixth column. Take volume one. You'll have to use the stool."

As she was directed, Alma stepped up onto the stool and stretched to the top shelf and removed the book.

"If you like the trilogy, he has more," Miss Lily said, adjusting her shawl. "Next time you come, bring some of your calligraphy."

"Yes, Miss Lily," Alma said, opening the door. "Goodbye."

As the days passed, Alma's story, which she had decided to call "The Dream-ary," took shape. Sammy borrowed his first dream card from Clio and put it under his pillow and was astounded by what happened. But the narrative, Alma realized, was already far too long.

Alma and Miss Lily talked together every time Alma came to do her copying. They discussed books and stories and history and myths and fables. Miss Lily gave pointers to Alma to improve her calligraphy, and Alma found that uncial was Miss Lily's favourite hand also.

"Do you know, Alma," Miss Lily mused on one of these occasions, "I think that in a former life you must have been a scribe. I can imagine you scraping vellum, mixing inks, shaping quills. You have books in your soul."

Alma didn't know what to say to that. She wasn't quite as frightened by Miss Lily as she used to be. Still, she decided not to ask what vellum was. She'd look it up when she got home.

Then one day Alma was copying a short note. "Dear Mr. Tyler," it said. "Many thanks for your kind wishes on my seventieth birthday. It was so kind of you to send me the lovely crystal ashtray."

Oh, no, Alma thought. I missed her birthday! When her duties were completed, she ran home, and as soon as her mother stepped into the apartment, she bubbled, "I missed Miss Lily's birthday! It was her seventieth. That's a special one, isn't it?"

"For heaven's sake, Alma, can't you for once let me get into the room before you bowl me over with words?" Clara complained, pulling off her waitress apron. She wore a uniform to work now, a green dress with a frilly white apron.

"Can I use some of the money I earn to buy her a present?" Alma went on. "I know her birthday's gone by, but still, Miss Lily has lent me a lot of books and she—"

"Slow down, girl," Clara begged. "Of course you can buy her a present. That's sweet of you."

"Can I go to the gift shop on Grafton Street? Can I go now?"

"That place charges too much, Alma."

"Well, could I go and look?"

"Don't be late for supper."

Alma spent ages in the gift shop, perusing the crystal, pottery, blankets woven from mohair and wool, bowls fashioned from exotic woods, jewellery and candlesticks of softly glowing pewter. It was the quilts she liked best, hand-stitched and vibrating with colour, but the prices were far, far beyond what she could pay. And then, as she turned to go, she spied a small pillow propped on an antique wooden chair by the door. The pillow, too, was quilted, and the quilter must have lived in Charlotte's Bight, because the little scenes depicted in the design made up of small squares were familiar to Alma: the lighthouse on East Point, the shells you could find on Little Harbour Beach on any summer's day, a dory cresting a wave, gulls and ships and more. And in the background the quilter had stitched the outline of a lady's slipper. Alma bought it with shaking hands, and raced home.

On Saturday morning, Alma surprised Miss Olivia by asking her, "Before I start work, may I speak to Miss Lily?"

Miss Olivia's thick eyebrows rose as she touched her beads and eyed the package Alma carried. "I'll see," she said, and she went down the hall and tapped lightly on the study door.

A few minutes later, Alma stood in the study, with Miss Olivia behind her, watching as Miss Lily struggled with the pink ribbon around the box. Miss Olivia moved toward the chair.

"Let me help you, Mother."

"I can manage," Miss Lily snapped, dropping the ribbon and, using her stiff red fingers like spades, sliding them under the tape holding the sea-blue wrapping paper, creating a ragged tear. Alma waited as Miss Lily then struggled with the box, a scowl on her face, her lips pressed together in frustration. With a snap, the tape parted and Miss Lily raised the lid.

"I'm sorry it's late, Miss Lily," Alma said. "Happy birthday. It's from my mother and me."

Sometimes, in the sky over the harbour, Alma would watch as the west wind pushed the heavy grey rain clouds away, allowing a bar of sun to burst through and illuminate the water, turning it instantly from slate grey to a warm, deep blue. That was what happened to Miss Lily's face when she lifted the quilted pillow from the box. Her scowl fled and her features softened. She said nothing, tracing the delicate stitching of the lady's slipper with her fingers.

Then she looked at Alma, and Alma realized there were tears slipping from Miss Lily's eyes, following the deep lines on her face.

"Thank you, Alma," she said, and her voice caught. She began to sob.

"Let's leave Miss Lily alone for a moment," Miss Olivia said, taking Alma's hand and tugging sharply. Alma followed her out, her mind churning, unsure how she should feel.

"I'm sorry," she began, "I didn't—"

"Oh, don't be sorry," Miss Olivia said, her usual businesslike tone absent. "Miss Lily's just a bit overcome. Why don't you get your work done and you can talk to her before you leave."

Alma sat at the desk, straight pen in hand, and copied the first letter, her ear cocked for any sound from the study. She worked through the correspondence, writing carefully, setting each letter aside to let the ink dry fully before clipping it to its envelope, shaping her letters while, as usual, her mind wandered. Why had Miss Lily been overcome with tears? she asked herself for the tenth or twelfth time. Didn't she like the pillow? Maybe it was an unwise choice. Alma felt a hot flush of embarrassment creep up her neck and she glanced up to see if Miss Olivia was by any chance standing in the doorway. What use would a little pillow be to someone like Miss Lily?

Alma hardly noticed the words of the next letter in the file. She had copied the opening salutation and begun the first paragraph before her breath caught in her throat and all thoughts of pillows fled from her mind. She stared at the line she had copied.

"Dear Hattie Scrivener,"

Thirteen

Alma swallowed deeply, her heart whumping in her chest, her mouth dry and scratchy. She was sure she would be unable to form a word, never mind a sentence. She stood just inside the door of the study. Olivia Chenoweth had closed the door softly and now Alma was alone with Miss Lily.

But it wasn't the Miss Lily Alma thought she knew—an unknown, scowly lady who lived in an old house by the harbour. Alma was in the same room as her very most favourite author!

That stupid pillow. A mistake. A bad present, too late for the birthday. What would RR Hawkins want with a little pillow made by an unknown quilter in a small, unimportant place like Charlotte's Bight?

Miss Lily sat with her gnarled hands resting like claws on the same pillow, one curled finger on the lighthouse, another seeming to point to the plovers on a sandy shore.

"Do forgive me, Alma," she began. "I don't know what came over me. I was overwhelmed by your kindness."

Alma opened her mouth but nothing came out.

"It's a lovely gift," Miss Lily went on. "I . . . it's especially precious to me because I used to quilt myself. I made my own designs and . . . well, that was some time ago. Now . . ."

She looked down at her hands, then at Alma's face, and Alma understood.

"I'm glad you like it, Miss Lily," she said.

The old strength returned to the woman's voice. "Why are you fidgeting so, Alma? Are you quite all right? You look pale. I apologize for upsetting you a while ago."

"I'm . . . I'm fine," Alma croaked. "Fine."

"Well, have you completed your work for this morning?" the writer asked, her tone businesslike once more.

"Yes, Miss Lily."

"Good. Hand me a cigarette and my holder, if you will, before you go."

Alma left the house, and as soon as she reached the sidewalk, she tore up the street, her feet squelching through the slush. Should I tell Mom? she asked herself. No, Mom won't understand. The truth was that Alma wanted to keep the delicious secret to herself, at least for a while, like a piece of sponge toffee melting slowly in her mouth.

As soon as Alma got home, she began another letter to RR Hawkins. This time, she didn't hold back. She wrote and wrote—about RR Hawkins's books and how much she loved them, about the questions she had always wanted to ask, but mostly about two things. Why, she asked politely and insistently, did you stop writing stories? Did you run out of ideas? Did you get sick and tired of fame?

The second thing Alma stressed was, I want to be a writer too, and now I'm writing a story for school, but it's much too long and I'm afraid I won't get it done in time. Maybe I won't be able to finish it at all. Do you have any suggestions?

"Dear Hattie Scrivener," came the reply a few weeks later,

Thank you for your latest. Forgive me if I do not respond to some of your questions, as they are of a personal nature. I'm sure that you are aware that I am an extremely private person and prefer to let my books speak for themselves.

As to why I have stopped writing, that too is a personal matter and a story that would take too long to relate.

I do hope you finish your story successfully, and if you will allow me a small piece of advice, you would do well to remember that success is a sword with two edges.

Yours sincerely,

Dear RR Hawkins,

Thank you for writing back to me so soon.

I don't blame you for not telling me why you stopped writing. It's none of my business, really.

But, please! couldn't you write just one more? Your books are so good! Nobody can write stories as good as yours.

"And one more thing," Alma added, repeating her second letter somewhat because RR Hawkins hadn't really said anything about "The Dream-ary,"

> *Could you give me some advice? I have*
> *written a story, or part of one, and now*
> *I'm stuck. Do . . . Did you ever get*
> *stuck? And if you did, what did you do*
> *to get unstuck? Could I send you my*
> *story so you could give me some ideas?*
> *Yours sincerely,*
> *Hattie Scrivener*

On the day she posted her letter, Alma sat in the front parlour of the house on Little Wharf Road, copying. The morning breeze wafted through the window, carrying birdsong like a fragrance from the maples across the street. Miss Olivia had slipped out to do a little shopping, leaving Alma alone with Miss Lily, something she had been doing more and more frequently over the winter and spring. Alma felt a flush of pride when she reminded herself that Olivia Chenoweth was entrusting her mother's safety to her.

"Alma!" she heard from the back of the house.

Alma jumped to her feet and dashed to the door of the study. She knocked softly. "Miss Lily?"

"Come."

When Alma opened the door, she could hardly believe her eyes.

"You're standing up!"

"Of course I'm standing up. I've dropped my walking stick," the old woman complained, as if Alma had personally knocked it from her hands. "Well, don't stand there gaping, Alma!"

Alma stooped and picked up the stick and handed it to Miss Lily.

"You've told me your favourite place in this town is the old harbour?"

"Yes, Miss Lily."

"Well, let's go down there and see what the fuss is about. We should go now, before Olivia returns and refuses to allow it."

"But—"

"You'll find my coat in the hall closet. And I'll need your help, Alma."

With Miss Lily using her walking stick in her right hand, her left on Alma's shoulder, they made their laborious way down the front steps and out onto the street, turning toward the harbour. The breeze off the ocean was fresh and chill, infused with the odours of kelp and fish and salt. Along the wharf, lobster traps were piled high and deep, awaiting the season's opening in a few weeks.

Alma walked slowly, careful not to upset the old woman's balance. I'm strolling along the shore with a famous author, she thought. She knows and I know, but she doesn't know I know! Alma giggled to herself.

"What's taken your fancy?" Miss Lily asked.

"Oh, nothing."

"Nobody laughs at nothing, Alma."

Alma showed Miss Lily the marina, and the shops and restaurants, some of which were being given a fresh coat of paint in preparation for the tourist season. A few residents walked their dogs along the quay or meandered arm in arm, soaking up the spring sun.

Soon, though, Miss Lily grew tired and asked Alma to take her home.

"We'll do that again sometime, shall we, Alma?" Miss Lily said as she carefully lowered herself into her chair and reached for her cigarette holder.

"Anytime you wish, Miss Lily," Alma replied. Miss Hawkins, she didn't say.

Fourteen

"_Dear_ Hattie Scrivener," Alma wrote—or, rather, copied—as rain fell softly onto the lawns and sidewalks outside the window on Little Wharf Road.

> *Thank you for your latest.*
>
> *I'm afraid I am unable to help you with your story. As you may imagine, I receive many requests such as you have made and cannot possibly respond to all of them. Therefore, in fairness, I reply to none.*
>
> *The only advice I can give is that you take your story to someone you trust, perhaps someone who loves to read as*

> *much as you do.*
> *Sincerely,*

Such was her disappointment that Alma put a little too much force behind the comma after "Sincerely" and made an ugy blot on the page. She sighed heavily, took a new sheet of creamy paper from its pigeonhole in the writing desk and began again. By the time she had finished the letter for the second time, a devilish smile creased her face.

I'll show *you*, RR Hawkins, she said to herself.

On the next Saturday morning, Alma and Miss Lily took another walk, this time with the knowledge and blessing of Miss Olivia, who gave Alma a broad, gap-toothed smile as they left the house. Alma watched the gulls wheeling above the harbour, wishing she could translate their sharp cries into human talk. Were they squawking about food? The people on the quay below? The sailboats tied to the jetties, rocking gently? Was there such a thing as seagull talk?

Alma had decided to follow RR Hawkins's advice, and the trusted friend she chose to ask for help was Miss Lily herself! She wondered if this would be a good time. Miss Lily sat on a park bench beside Alma, her pale, wrinkled face turned up to the warm morning sun. She wore an uncharacteristically colourful dress under her black shawl, and cotton gloves. Alma knew without having been told that Miss Lily wore the gloves to hide her swollen red fingers.

Alma made a decision. "Um, Miss Lily?"

"Yes, dear," the writer replied without opening her eyes or turning her face toward Alma.

"I was wondering if I could ask you a question."

"Alma, don't wonder if you could. If you have something to ask, ask."

Alma reminded herself that Miss Lily hated indirectness. "I need help with a story I'm writing for Miss McAllister," Alma blurted.

Miss Lily nodded. "And who is Miss McAllister?"

"My teacher. We have to hand in a story by next Monday and there's a prize for the best one and I'm stuck on mine and I'm afraid it will be too long."

The pale lids on the old eyes opened, then closed again immediately. "And what makes you think I can help?"

Because you know more about stories than

anyone in the world, Alma wanted to say. Because you're the best, better than Shakespeare I bet, even though I've never read any of his plays.

"Because you love to read books, just like me. Only you've read a lot more." And I trust you, she didn't add.

Miss Lily opened her eyes and turned to Alma. "What is the problem, then, exactly?"

When Miss Lily said "exactly" that was *exactly* what she meant. No beating around the bush, or shilly-shallying, as Olivia Chenoweth would say.

"I'm stuck. I can't figure out how to end it."

"Be good enough to fix me a ciggie," Miss Lily directed, awkwardly handing Alma the cloth bag that had been resting in her lap.

Lately, she had begun to allow Alma to fix a cigarette in the ivory holder for her and to hold the ornate lighter to the end while she puffed the cigarette to life. "Tell me the story," she said, smoke pouring from her nostrils.

Beginning slowly and nervously but gaining confidence as she described Sammy's first dream, Alma related the tale she had been working on for months. "And that's as far as I got," she concluded.

Miss Lily laughed. "The Dream-ary. What a wonderful idea. I wish I'd thought of it myself."

Miss Lily's laugh, Alma thought, was as rare as . . . well, she hardly ever laughed, so the story must be good. Alma felt a surge of pleasure.

"So you don't know how to end it," Miss Lily said.

"No."

"Well, I don't think that's the problem at all," said the old woman, giving Alma the cigarette holder.

Alma pinched off the butt like a professional and shook it from the holder. She picked it up off the cobblestones and deposited it in a receptacle beside the bench. She waited for the author to go on.

"While you were telling me about Sammy, his family and his dreams," Miss Lily said in her strong, deep voice, which seemed to Alma to be even stronger now, "you mentioned three times that you think his story is too long."

Miss Lily paused, but Alma was thinking. She said *his* story and family and dreams, as if Sammy was a real person. Then Alma realized Miss Lily was waiting for her to say something.

"Yes. Miss McAllister said it could only be five pages or less. I'm already at page—"

"That sounds like something a teacher would say," Miss Lily rumbled. Then, louder, "Perhaps you're so worried about the story being over-length that you won't let it tell itself."

"'Tell itself'?"

"Yes. Now listen carefully. You think of it as your story because you are writing it. That's understandable, but wrong. Every story, especially one as good as this one, has its own life. It has its own length. You cannot impose a length on it. The story, once begun, must run its course. I think you'll find that if you forget about what Miss McAllister said and let yourself relax, the story will tell you its own ending. Then you can write it down. Don't try to control it. Understand?"

"Yes. Well, I think so."

"Never mind 'I think so.' Do you or don't you?"

"Yes."

"Good. Now, I will give you a little hint and that's all. You must do the rest. At the beginning of the story, Sammy is upset because he thinks his parents didn't plan to have a child. He feels unwanted."

"Yes."

"From what you've told me, that problem isn't resolved yet."

Alma furrowed her brow and thought for a moment. "No, it isn't."

"Good. Now let's walk back before my daughter sends the Coast Guard to find us."

Alma sat in her room, on the rug, using the couch as a desktop. The tea things were laid out on the kitchen table for her mother's return. Through the ceiling came the throb of a bodhran drum and a melody carried on a tin whistle, backed by fiddle and guitar. Alma went over what Miss Lily had said, about the story finding its own length, then Miss McAllister's assignment, repeated at least three times, "If your story is too long, I will mark it of course, but it cannot earn more than a C. And it will be disqualified for the prize."

Alma doodled for a moment, forming her name and "RR Hawkins" and "Clara" and "Sammy," alternating Carolingian letters with half-uncials. The story is already lots too long, she reminded herself for the umpteenth time. And I don't have time to do another. So I'm going to finish it and hand it in.

And I won't win the prize. My story can't even be in the contest.

But I'm going to write it anyway, and make it the best I possibly can, she said to herself. She found that as soon as she stopped worrying about the length, her ideas flowed again.

Fifteen

The classroom shimmered with energy and buzzed with illicit whispering. Miss McAllister pointed to the ten arithmetic problems she had written on the blackboard and commanded her pupils to begin. Feet shuffled on the floorboards, pencils twiddled unproductively, figures were written on foolscap and abandoned, the number of requests to go to the pencil sharpener on the wall by the door was ten times the usual.

Outside, the leaves on the trees and shrubs hung limp in the fiery afternoon air. The fragrance of tulips and irises rose from the flowerbeds and through the open windows to tantalize the pupils with the promise of long, languid days free of letters and numbers and assignments.

It was the second-last day of school. Alma looked at the clock once more. Fifteen minutes until the story contest winner was announced. At recess, in the schoolyard, Alma had heard Louise Arsenault whisper to her covey of admirers that she was to win. Her mother, who wrote poems and had them published in the Charlotte's Bight *Herald*, had helped her, even though it was against the rules. And, Louise hardly needed to add, Miss McAllister liked her best.

Out of the running herself, Alma hoped anyone *but* Louise would take the prize. But, she admitted, Louise was probably right.

Finally, Miss McAllister consulted what Alma called the "upside-down watch" that hung from a brooch below her collar. She stood, smoothed her dress over her thin hips, and moved slowly to the metal filing cabinet. She pulled open the middle drawer and removed a bundle of papers. Clutching them against her chest, she walked to the centre of the area before the blackboard and announced, "Very well, you may put away your arithmetic."

A great shuffling of feet, rustling of papers, squeaking of hinges as desktops rose up and thumped down, followed the teacher's words. When quiet returned, each pupil sat, as instructed over the year—in some cases, like Lenny Grant, time and time again—with hands clasped and resting motionless on the desktop.

"This year," Miss McAllister began, her voice bubbling with enthusiasm, "we have a number of wonderful stories."

There was a surge of shifting-in-the-seat, glances and smiles. Miss McAllister waited until calm was restored. "And, for the first time, we have three honourable mentions in addition to the winner."

Another wave of fidgeting swept through the room. When the waters were tranquil once again, Miss McAllister called out the names and the titles. Bobby Kirkpatrick, for "The Storm at Midnight," Alice McAskill for "My Best Friend" and Agnes Moore for "The Christmas Gift," which, Miss McAllister added, was quite similar to O. Henry's "The Gift of the Magi," but never mind.

Alma hardly listened. She burned with an alternating current of envy and shame—jealous of the pupils who received honourable mention, ashamed of herself for a feeling she knew was unworthy. She should be glad for her successful classmates, but she wasn't. If only my name had been mentioned, she thought; if only I could win.

"And the winner of this year's prize," Miss McAllister chirped, "for her story—"

Louise Arsenault, Alma saw, had her palms pressed against the sides of her face and her eyes were afire with anticipation. Her pals Samantha and Polly stared at her. Then, in an instant, the light in her face disappeared.

" 'The Littlest Hero,' is—"

Alma watched as Louise lowered her hands, her face tight as she struggled to control her disappointment. Louise forced herself to smile, and at that moment Alma felt sorry for her.

"Jennifer Andrews!" Miss McAllister almost sang the name. "Come up here, Jennifer."

The waters around Louise chopped and churned as her followers whispered their shock and outrage. Jennifer won't have a pleasant walk home, Alma thought.

"Attention," Miss McAllister said. She had presented Jennifer with a brand-new dictionary and the winner had carried it to her seat, beaming.

"There was one sour note in the contest this year," Miss McAllister intoned, her voice suddenly sombre. "In spite of my repeating the directions several times, one of you wilfully refused to follow them. This person submitted a story that was more than three times the allowed length."

Something inside Alma lurched, leaving a sinking feeling of nausea. Don't say my name, she chanted inside her head. Her throat and face burned with shame. Don't tell them it was me.

"Alma Neal," Miss McAllister said, "ruined her chances by refusing to be guided by the rules."

Every face turned toward Alma.

"Now, we must learn from this unfortunate example," the teacher admonished. "Alma, your story was good—quite good, really—but it was too long."

"It wasn't!"

Alma was shocked by her own outburst. A look of malicious satisfaction crossed Louise Arsenault's freckled face. A few pupils tittered as the rest continued to stare at her, wide-eyed at her rebellion.

"I'm afraid it was, Alma. You know that as well as I. Now—"

"I asked a famous author—the best author in the world—and she told me you can't make a story fit an assignment. She said every story will find its own—"

"Well," Miss McAllister's voice rose as she interrupted, "I wasn't aware that any renowned writers lived in Charlotte's Bight, so I don't know who this so-called author might be. But obviously her—"

"It was RR Hawkins! She's my friend. She told me! And she knows more than you about—"

Alma's words dried up instantly. She sat, scarcely able to believe what she had just said. Her breath came in gasps. Her legs threatened to give out as she rose from her seat and stumbled down the aisle past gaping faces. By the time she got through the classroom door, she was running.

When Alma was a little girl her mother had taught her about conscience. "It's a little bit of God in you," Clara had explained. "A kind of voice. It doesn't tell you what to do, but it lets you know if what you've done or want to do is right or wrong. And because it's God helping you, you can trust the voice."

Alma had wondered where inside her this voice resided. Was it in her chest, where her heart was? Or inside her head, nestled in her brain? If it was a voice, perhaps it lived in her ear.

After her outburst in Miss McAllister's classroom, the tempest in Alma's conscience drove her along the street the way the northwest wind harried the fallen autumn leaves along the sidewalks. Alma ran until she arrived gasping at the alley door of the Liffey Pub. She was so agitated she needed both hands to guide her key into the lock. She slammed the door behind her and dashed to her room. She fell onto the couch, clutched handfuls of her hair, screaming silently. Her head throbbed and ached. Her chest rose and fell like an ailing pump.

What have I done? she moaned repeatedly, knowing the answer full well. She had given away the biggest secret she had ever carried, the most colossal private confidence in Charlotte's Bight. Or in the whole country. Or in the world. She had betrayed her friend, the person she admired most, the woman who represented all she wanted to be. And for what? Because she was envious of a prize, and hurt because her teacher had singled her out for criticism and ridicule. No wonder Miss

McAllister doesn't like me, Alma raged. I'm not worth liking.

The storm swept into Alma's body, bringing a fever, and when her mother arrived for the supper break, Alma was half-delirious, mumbling to herself, her skin filmed with sweat. She was fiery hot, then cold, then hot again. She was barely conscious of her mother putting her to bed, of the sweet taste of honey and tea. She ran on incoherently about betrayal and guilt and broken friendship.

Alma was hardly aware of the doctor's visit and the conversation behind the closed door of her room, the closing of the kitchen door, the weight of her mother's body on the edge of the bed, the cool damp cloth on her forehead. In the morning, her fever ebbed, but she felt unconnected to her surroundings when her mother questioned her, holding another mug of tea to Alma's dry lips.

"I've called the Chenoweth house and told them you can't come this afternoon," Clara said.

"Hawkins," Alma muttered.

"And I've telephoned the school. It's a shame you'll miss the last day," Clara rattled on. "What a time to come down with a spring cold. How did the story contest turn out?"

Alma was overcome by a squall of tears.

"What happened?" Clara demanded. "Tell me, Alma."

"I . . . I told on her," Alma sobbed. "I ruined everything. She'll hate me now."

"Who, Alma? For heaven's sake, sit up and control yourself. There, that's better. Wipe your face with the cloth. Now, who are you talking about?"

"Miss Lily. Miss McAllister criticized my story and—"

Try as she might, Alma could make no sense. Her words chased each other, throwing up dust and confusion; and finally Clara gave up. She took away the empty mug.

"Lie down, Alma, and try to get to sleep."

As Alma fell back on the bed she heard, "And I'm going to telephone that school and find out what's going on."

Three days passed before Alma was able to rise from her bed, and the first thing she did was turn her Hawkins novels around on the shelves. The seven gold *RRH*s on the spines had glowed accusingly, making it impossible for her to look in their direction.

Alma was relieved that school was over for the summer and she didn't have to go back and face her teacher or her classmates. But the house on Little Wharf Road seemed to hover above her every waking moment, glowering with menace. Sooner or later RR Hawkins would hear that Alma had revealed her secret, and she would be furious with Alma and never want to see her again. Miss Lily might even have to move away to preserve her privacy. In any case, there would be no more calligraphy lessons, no more walks to the harbour, no more quiet conversations before the fire. She had been lucky enough to meet her favourite author, just as she had always dreamed, but she had betrayed her. I can never be a writer now, Alma thought. I don't deserve to be.

It was more than a week after Alma fell ill— a week during which she refused to go outside, even for a minute—before she was able to explain things to her mother. They sat at the kitchen table, as they always did when there was something important to discuss, and before them were cups of hot tea.

"I found out," Alma began, "that Miss Lily is really RR Hawkins. By accident," she added hastily. "I didn't snoop or anything." Alma had long ago decided that writing to Miss Lily through her publisher wasn't prying.

"You're not serious! Honest and true? The writer you did your project on?"

Alma nodded. "But she never knew that I discovered her. Remember, Mom? She hid away from people, her fans and newspaper reporters and teachers. All her mail went to her publisher first, so no one would find out where she lived."

"So you went over there twice a week, knowing who she was, and she never twigged."

"I thought she'd get mad if I told her I knew."

"Then how did the secret come out?"

Swallowing hard, Alma related the events in the classroom the day before school ended for the summer, her eyes on her mother's face, alert for the look of disappointment she knew would come. And come it did.

"You told the secret because the teacher criticized your story," Clara concluded.

Alma fixed her eyes on the bottom of her empty teacup.

"You wanted to lift yourself in Miss McAllister's eyes—and your schoolmates' eyes—by revealing someone else's secret."

Alma nodded again.

"You'll have to tell her, you know."

Alma felt the tears hot on her face. "Mom! I can't! I couldn't face her!"

Clara's jaw had set, the way Alma hated, because it always meant her mother was about to make her do something she'd rather not. "I understand why you did it, Alma," she said. "But you can't walk by it as if it didn't happen."

Sixteen

As if it had joined in Alma's dismay, the sky opened up and poured rain on Charlotte's Bight for five days in a row, the low dark clouds turning day to an unpleasant twilight, battering the town with thunder. Water dripped continuously from the leaky eaves-trough above Alma's window, and a fitful wind dashed pellets of rain against the glass. Alma found she could no longer pass the time reading, because stories had lost their appeal. Her calligraphy pen lay untouched on a shelf. She spent her time sprawled on her bed, doz-ing fitfully, or tidying up the house, sweeping floors that didn't need to be swept, re-organizing dishes on the kitchen shelves. She washed down the hot plate and counter once a day. She pushed herself through aimless work, punishing herself with boring tasks.

On Sunday she helped her mother with the laundry, and, later, shoved the cart up and down the grocery-store aisles. She didn't ask even once to visit the Turnaround. When Clara and she returned home, stepping around the big puddles of dirty brown water in the alley, and put away the groceries, Alma offered to do the ironing, then went to lie down without any lunch. She lay for hours, listening to her mother humming to herself in the kitchen, the sparrows squabbling at the eaves, watching the gingham curtains lift and fall like waves in the warm breeze.

And then she heard a sound that froze her heart. Two voices, outside in the alley, growing louder and clearer every minute.

Alma jumped from the bed and ran to the window, looking out in time to see two women at her door. There was a knock. Alma's breath caught in her throat. Her heart skipped and thumped. The door creaked, voices exchanged greetings, the door clapped shut. Alma stood at the window, clutching a curtain, wondering what to do.

"Alma," her mother called. "Come into the kitchen, please. We have visitors."

Alma stood fixed to the spot, breathing through her open mouth.

"Alma," Clara called again with the slight edge to her voice that signified displeasure. Alma took a deep breath and made her way to the kitchen.

Miss Olivia, in a summer dress with a pattern of black-eyed Susans, a string of green beads around her neck, sat at the kitchen table, her round face expressionless. Beside her sat Miss Lily, one gloved hand on her walking stick, her mouth turned down at the corners, her piercing eyes on Alma, as if accusing her. Alma's mother stood at the hot plate watching the kettle.

"Set the table for tea, please, Alma," her mother said formally. "And it might be polite to greet Mrs. Chenoweth and Miss Hawkins."

Alma's first words sounded like a croak. "Hello, Miss Lily. Hello, Miss Olivia."

She stood like a post, her arms at her sides, her hands clenched, waiting. Before Miss Lily, a bulging cloth bag sat on the kitchen table.

The two women returned her greetings, then Miss Lily said, "Your mother was kind enough to inform us that you've not been feeling well, Alma, so we thought we'd drop by to see how you are."

"Miss Lily walked the whole way," Miss Olivia put in, earning a scowl from her mother.

"The tea things," Clara prodded.

Alma went to the shelves, returning with four matching cups and saucers rattling in her hands. She put out the sugar bowl and milk jug.

"Sit down, Alma," Clara said.

Alma did as she was told, folding her hands in her lap. In a way, she decided, she was relieved. Now she would face her punishment. It would be awful, but it would be over soon. Finally.

"Alma," Miss Lily began, "I'm very disappointed in you—"

But before the writer could utter another word, Alma burst out, "I'm sorry, Miss Lily! I'm sorry! I shouldn't have done it! It's all my fault. It's just that Miss McAllister didn't believe I knew—" And she stopped abruptly, aware that she was about to make an excuse. There was no excuse.

The full weight of her loss fell upon her and Alma began to sob. How she had loved going to Miss Lily's house, copying her letters in the parlour knowing full well whose correspondence she dealt with, taking walks with the writer and talking about books, even fixing her cigarette for her and lighting it, even, Alma thought, Miss Olivia's gap-toothed smile.

"Alma," Miss Lily cut in, her deep, gravelly voice more gravelly than usual. "You misunderstand me. Your mother has explained what happened at school. I'm not pleased at all that you brought me into the matter. But I'm disappointed that you thought me such a poor friend that I would hold a grudge against you."

Alma heard the words but they rattled around in her head without forming a thought. She sat staring at the author, uncomprehending.

"I . . . but . . . I'm sorry, Miss Lily." And then Alma put the words together. "You mean . . . But I—"

Clara put the teapot in the middle of the table. "Pour the tea, Alma."

Alma attempted to lift the teapot, but her hands shook.

"Perhaps you'd allow me," Miss Olivia said, taking the pot from Alma's hands.

Alma could scarcely believe what she had just heard. Miss Lily didn't hate her after all. But how could she not?

"And since you know the truth about me," Miss Lily went on sternly, "I'd like you to have something." She pushed the bag across the table. "I know you have copies already, but perhaps you'd prefer these."

A broad smile graced Miss Olivia's face as she spooned sugar into her cup and stirred.

Alma looked at her mother. Clara smiled and nodded. Alma pulled on the drawstrings of the bag. It was full of books. Seven of them, brand new, and identically bound in rich maroon leather. She opened one and held it up to her nose. The book gave off the fragrance of leather and ink and fine-quality paper. A thin gold ribbon attached to the binding served as a bookmark. On the spine of the book, in gold letters, was printed *Into the Shadows*, and under it, *RRH*. Inside the book, on the title page, in jittery, scrawly handwriting, was, "To my friend and fellow writer, Alma." Alma checked the other six books. Each one had the same inscription, written by Miss Lily herself.

As the afternoon wore on and cup after cup of tea was consumed, Alma was struck by surprise after surprise. RR Hawkins was a recluse, she learned, but not obsessed with secrecy. She wanted to live a private life, would not give interviews or meet with her readers, but she had never tried to run away or live secretly, as Alma had always thought. She simply wanted to be left alone. She and Miss Olivia had moved to Charlotte's Bight because they had grown tired of the city. The selling of their house in Boston had been very complicated owing to a buyer who reneged on the deal at the last minute.

As Miss Lily explained these facts, Alma felt as if she were a musty old attic, shut up for years and years, dusty and mouldy, and then someone had opened a window, letting in a sweet, cool breeze. By the time Miss Lily and Miss Olivia rose from the table and went to the outside door, Alma was beginning to feel herself again. And after they went through the door, Miss Olivia popped her head back inside.

"Alma, may we expect you next Tuesday at the regular time? We have quite a bit of correspondence waiting."

Alma looked at her mother, who nodded. "Yes," she said.

"And Miss Lily forgot to say that, if it's all right with you, she'd like to read your story."

Alma nodded.

"You may bring it with you on Tuesday. And one more thing," Miss Olivia added, her voice falling to a whisper. "Before you came, Miss Lily hadn't gone for a walk in over a year."

With that, she closed the door quietly behind her.

Alma went to her room and sat on the edge of her bed, taking up the new RRH novels one at a time and touching the gold letters, rereading the inscription penned by the best author ever. So many questions had been answered.

Except one, she said to herself. She looked at the name written in black ink underneath her own, the letters wavering, scrawled by an arthritic hand.

Why did you stop writing? —

Seventeen

$\mathscr{A}$lma remembered almost nothing of the farm where she was born, but sometimes images would flash in her mind like the sun on glass when she opened the window of her room. Lounging on her bed one hot, sticky morning, daydreaming with her eyes closed, she saw roads of red dirt rising and falling as they crossed a rolling green countryside of farms and woodlots. The Queen Anne's lace, goldenrod, St. John's wort and vetch trimmed the shoulders of the roads with white and yellow and purple. Fields stretched to the sky. The potatoes were well along, their flowers blown and faded; the barley was a shimmering green, the oats toasty-gold, plump ears nodding in the breeze. Later, as she strolled down Little Wharf Road on her way to the Chenoweth house, she tried to recall what it had been like living on the farm, but she couldn't.

The routine at the Chenoweth house was unchanged by summer. True, Miss Olivia and Miss Lily had exchanged their heavy dark dresses and shawls for cotton and gingham, the fireplace was swept and inactive, and there was a brand-new electric table fan in the parlour for the hottest days, but the letter writing continued. It had taken Alma two weeks to catch up on the correspondence that had awaited her in the bulging folder on the desk. Now she went "to work," as her mother called it, whenever she wanted.

And, most times, if the weather was fine, she and Miss Lily went for a walk. Leaning on her walking stick, the author took each step stiffly and with care. At times they talked. At others, they walked silently and companionably along the sidewalks of Charlotte's Bight. Miss Lily, Alma had learned, was a great believer in silence. "Do not speak," she once commanded Alma, "unless you can improve upon tranquility." Alma hadn't been quite sure what the author meant, but she got the idea.

On this day, they had gone to the park by the harbour and taken a bench with a view of the river mouth, where the tide ran strong, carrying jellyfish and strings of kelp upriver. The bench stood under an oak tree. Miss Lily sat on the shady side.

"Are you looking forward to commencing school again?" she asked, breaking Alma's reverie. "There are two weeks left of your summer."

"Sort of," Alma replied. "I've got Mr. Strachan this year. He's strict. And he always has speckles of dandruff on the shoulders of his jacket. And he wears the same tie, every day. That's what Robbie Thornton says."

Alma saw a smile begin to form at the corners of Miss Lily's lips. "Does this Mr. Strachan allow you to write stories?"

"I don't know. I guess so. But he doesn't have penmanship."

"In any case, I hope you'll continue to write stories on your own."

"Oh, I will. I started a new one yesterday."

Alma's confidence in her writing had blossomed when Miss Lily had told her she thought "The Dream-ary" is wonderful. "I love it," Miss Lily had said. Alma had glowed with pleasure.

Imagine, having your story praised by your favourite real live writer. Later she began to doubt herself. Maybe Miss Lily was just being polite. Then Alma reminded herself that Miss Lily was very blunt and honest and straightforward. No, Alma had concluded, if Miss Lily thought my story was no good she would have said so.

As they sat on the bench, listening to the cries of the gulls wheeling over the estuary, the laughter of little kids on the swings behind them, the faint notes from the old man playing the fiddle over by the ice cream stand, Alma screwed up her courage.

"Miss Lily, could I ask you something?"

"You just did," the writer replied. "Remind me why it's silly to ask someone if you can ask her something."

"Because you can't un-ask a question," Alma recited.

"Fine. Now go ahead."

"Why did you stop writing books?"

Miss Lily turned her head in the direction of the estuary, where a sailboat was passing through the swing bridge, its sails furled, its motor *chug-chug-chugging* as it headed toward the gap. She stared for a long time. Alma began to fidget. She had upset Miss Lily. After all, it was none of her business why the writer had abandoned her vocation.

"It is difficult to explain," Miss Lily replied, turning to Alma. "When I began the Centreworld books, I had no plans to continue once the trilogy was complete. By the time the third novel was published, I had conceived the idea for Alterworld, which was, as you know, an even larger project."

"Four volumes," Alma said.

"By the time I had finished my seventh book, fourteen—no, fifteen—years had passed. Fifteen years of extremely difficult, concentrated effort. I was tired."

Alma kept silent.

"And," Miss Lily continued after a minute, "as you know, I didn't at all appreciate the public attention. In particular, those who felt that they could delve into my past or write articles pretending to know everything about my personal life and my work."

Alma knew a little about Miss Lily's past, but she said nothing, willing the author to continue, using her silence to encourage more talk.

"But the main thing, I think, was that I had simply lost my passion for telling stories. That's something you know about, Alma, the passion, because you have it."

Alma thought she knew what Miss Lily meant, but she wasn't sure. "Tell me what it's like," she said. "Please."

"Perhaps," Miss Lily began, "it is, above all things, lonely. So many hours by oneself, lost in research or imaginings. Then there is the lack of understanding. So many people seem to think that all one has to do is find an idea for a story and write it down. They talk of inspiration as if it replaced grinding toil, the wrestling with ideas and character and narrative structure, the revising, the arguments with editors. And worst of all, the corroding self-doubt that will not go away no matter how well received the books are."

Miss Lily looked away again.

"All of which sounds like a complaint," she went on, "but I don't mean it that way. What gets us through is the thrill of making something out of nothing. It's the passion to tell the story that means so much to us."

Miss Lily seemed to run out of energy with her last sentence. She swallowed and looked again toward the estuary. A fresh breeze swept through the gap, cool and salty. A fishing boat was crossing the harbour, leaving a creamy wake behind.

Alma thought of her own excitement when an idea for a story slipped into her head and began to make room for itself, like a tenant in an apartment where she plans to stay for a long time. The thrill that swelled as the narrative grew and took form. The sense of satisfaction when the tale appeared on the page in Alma's cursive uncials.

"Don't you miss it?" she asked.

Miss Lily shrugged her shoulders. But the look on her face, Alma thought, said *Yes.*

"Do you think you'll ever get it back?" Alma persisted, but she saw that Miss Lily had finished. Her face, which had brightened moments earlier, seemed to close in again, stiff and wrinkled.

"There was a time, a long time, when I would have said no to that question. Now, I'm not so sure. At any rate, help me to my feet. You've worn me out with your prattling, Alma Neal."

They made their way up Little Wharf Road, the afternoon sun on their shoulders. Alma was thinking. Miss Lily had hinted that she might regain the passion she had described. Did that mean things had changed? Would RR Hawkins write again?

Eighteen

"<u>D</u>ear RR Hawkins," Alma wrote in her awkward Hattie Scrivener hand. "I am writing to make a confession to you."

Alma stopped to consider her words carefully. She had decided, after that day in the park with Miss Lily, that she ought to tell the truth about Hattie Scrivener.

"I am not who you think I am," she put down. She stopped again. Maybe it isn't such a good idea to be honest, she thought, placing her pen on the kitchen table. After all, honesty could hurt people sometimes, like when your best friend asked you if you liked her new blouse and you didn't and you wanted to tell her she looked hideous but you knew that would hurt her feelings but if you didn't tell her the truth she'd wear the horrible blouse and people would laugh at her and it would be your fault and—

Alma shook her head and picked up her fountain pen again. Such thinking was too confusing. Since Miss Lily had been so open with her about the most—or one of the most—important things in her life, her writing, then Alma couldn't go on deceiving her. Miss Lily had been dictating letters to a girl who didn't exist, and no matter how Alma looked at it, that wasn't fair.

"I am really someone you know," Alma continued.

> *My name is not Hattie Scrivener. And this isn't my handwriting. I am Alma Neal, and I'm very sorry for deceiving you, but, you see, I had to find out if you were really my favourite author. I hope you can forgive me.*
>   *Sincerely,*
>   *Alma Neal (Hattie Scrivener)*

On Thursday afternoon after school, Alma took the letter to the Chenoweth house. She tapped on the door and let herself in. At the end of July, Miss Olivia had told Alma she needn't wait; she should rap loudly with the knocker and enter the house.

Alma didn't see Miss Lily that day, and Miss Olivia appeared only for a moment, looking less cheerful than usual, and very busy. Miss Lily was feeling a little under the weather, she said. So Alma copied the letters that had been left for her in the file and, on her way out, laid her Hattie letter on the table in the hall.

Saturday morning was dreary and chilly, with low clouds and a damp breeze out of the north-east—a sign that bad weather lurked over the horizon. Alma had breakfast with her mother, who looked tired and drawn after a very late night at the Liffey.

"Take your raincoat and umbrella," Clara said as Alma slipped into the "new" autumn jacket that her mother had found at the Salvation Army thrift store. "It looks like dirty weather. I'm going back to bed for a bit."

The dry leaves rattled on the tossing branches as Alma made her way down Little Wharf Road, the wind on the side of her face.

She hurried up the path and banged the brass knocker and pushed open the door.

"Hello, Miss Lily. Hello, Miss Olivia," she called out, hanging her jacket on the rack by the door, taking in the fragrance of warm biscuits and coffee and fried bacon.

Miss Olivia called back a greeting from the kitchen, where the rattle of dishes told Alma that the breakfast washing-up was in progress. Alma entered the sitting room. In the middle of "her" desk was an envelope. She recognized the spidery, unsteady handwriting immediately. "To Alma."

Should she read it now? Or wait until her work was done? Alma opened the folder. There were three letters to copy. She put aside the envelope with her name on it and flipped open the inkwell lid. A half-hour later, she had completed her duties.

She sat back in her chair. Should she read her letter here? Or wait until she got home?

Alma decided to take it back to her room. She stuffed the envelope into the pocket of her jacket and went into the kitchen. Miss Olivia sat at the table, four or five small bottles of brown glass before her. She opened a bottle, shook pills into the palm of her hand, counted them and replaced them in the bottle, then made a note on a small pad.

"I'm finished for today, Miss Olivia," Alma said. She was trying hard to think of an excuse so that she wouldn't have to talk to Miss Lily.

"All right, dear," Olivia Chenoweth said. "I'm afraid Mother won't be able to speak with you today. She doesn't feel awfully well."

"Oh," Alma said, relieved, but pricked by a pang of guilt. "I hope she's better soon."

"I'm sure she will be."

"Well, goodbye, then."

"Dear Hattie Scrivener," Alma read, curled up on the couch in her room as the wind blustered outside the window. "Thank you for your most recent letter. Looking back, I recall that we have been corresponding for some months, some five or six letters, and all that time, you now admit, you were someone else."

Alma felt a little sick to her stomach, the way she always did when she knew she had been caught doing something wrong. She looked up from the page at the new leather-bound novels given to her by RR Hawkins. I've done it again, she thought. I've ruined everything. Why did I have to confess? I should have written one last letter as Hattie Scrivener and let it go at that.

She didn't want to finish the letter, to read the criticism she deserved, to hear disappointment shouting through the wavery handwriting. But she looked back to the page.

"I myself have a confession to make," the letter went on.

> *You see, I knew all along it was you, Alma. How did I know, you are now asking yourself as you read my very poorly written words.*
>
> *In the first place, I am aware that scrivener means writer, the vocation to which you have long aspired. Secondly, your letters were mailed from Charlotte's Bight, as indicated by the cancellation stamp imprinted by the post office. Thirdly, you must have forgotten that you told me long ago that your favourite name is Hattie. Remember, Alma, I used to make up stories for a living!*
>
> *Dear Alma, someday you will be a wonderful writer, but you will never be a successful criminal!*

Yours very sincerely,
Miss Lily (RR Hawkins)

P. S. I shall expect you and your mother
for tea on Sunday. I have something very
important to discuss with you.

Nineteen

"And what's this important thing, do you think?" Clara asked the next morning as she sprinkled water onto a pillowcase before ironing it.

"I don't know, Mom. She said she wanted to talk to you and me."

Alma hadn't told her mother about the letter. She pretended the invitation had come when she was at the Chenoweth house the day before.

"Probably something to do with your job," Clara guessed. "Maybe you're getting a raise," she said, smiling.

I don't care about that, Alma told herself. I just hope Miss Lily isn't mad at me for tricking her—trying to trick her—about Hattie Scrivener.

That afternoon, the sun finally broke through, reflecting brilliantly on the pearls of rain on the grass and trees and faded flowers in the gardens along Little Wharf Road. Alma and her mother, dressed for tea, walked slowly, enjoying the warmth of the day.

Alma's stomach churned. What was the "important thing"? she wondered once again. Was it good-important or bad-important? Alma was thinking about how much she hated uncertainty when her mother knocked on the door. Since it wasn't a workday but a social call, Alma didn't enter immediately.

The door opened suddenly to reveal Miss Olivia. "Oh," she burst out. "Oh!" Miss Olivia looked as if she had been wrestling with a ghost. Her face was ashen and drawn, her eyes blazing, her hair unkempt. "Come in! Come in!" she exclaimed. "I'm on the telephone. It's Mother." And, leaving the door open, she rushed back inside.

Alma followed her mother into the house. In the kitchen, Miss Olivia spoke into the telephone, nodding, raising her hand to her cheek, shaking her head.

"Something's happened to Miss Lily," Clara said.

"Yes, yes, all right," Miss Olivia said into the telephone. "I'll be there as soon as I can. Goodbye."

She hung up and placed her hand on her chest, as if to control her breathing. She sank into a chair.

"Miss Olivia, what's happened?" Clara asked softly.

"It's Mother. She's at the hospital. Oh, what shall I do?"

Clara turned to Alma. "Alma, put the kettle on," she commanded. "Do you know where everything is?"

She meant the tea things. "I . . . I think so," Alma said.

Alma's mother shucked off her coat and took one of the chairs. "Miss Olivia, tell me what happened," she said, leaning forward.

As Alma, still in her jacket, filled the kettle and lit the gas, took down the teapot from the cupboard and spooned tea into it, Miss Olivia reported that her mother had been unable to rise from her bed that morning. Though awake, she seemed unaware of where she was, and wouldn't—or couldn't—speak.

"I telephoned for the ambulance," Miss Olivia related, twisting her hanky in her hands.

"They wouldn't let me accompany Mother. I had just called them when you arrived. Oh, it was an agony waiting here, unable to be with her, wondering if—"

Alma laid out three cups and poured the boiling water into the teapot, hoping that hot tea was really the magical cure-all her mother always said it was.

"They say I can see her now," Miss Olivia concluded, winding down a little. Then she made to get to her feet. "I should be—"

"Take a little tea first," Clara said, putting her hand on Miss Olivia's arm. She pushed the milk and sugar toward her. "Did they tell you anything?"

"Only that Mother is stable," Miss Olivia said, sitting down. "Whatever that means. She's in Emergency." She spooned sugar into her cup, added milk, stirred slowly, her hand trembling.

A dreadful cloud settled on Alma as she began to take in what was happening. The hospital! A person could die! She felt tears on her face.

"Mom!" she cried. "Is Miss Lily going to—?"

"Oh, you poor girl!" Miss Olivia sprang to life. She got up and rushed to Alma, put her arms around her shoulders, held her. "I'm sure Mother will be all right."

Alma's sobs hit her like punches. She tried, but couldn't stop her tears. It was her mother who said, "Come, come, Alma. Get hold of yourself. It does no good to cry."

"I should be getting to the hospital," Miss Olivia said, releasing Alma. "I need to get some things together."

"Let us give you a hand," Clara said. "And Miss Olivia, forgive me, but you may want to, er, spruce yourself up a bit before you go."

"Yes, yes, you're right. Thank you."

Alma and her mother drank their tea. "What do you think will happen, Mom?" Alma asked, wiping her eyes with the back of her hand.

"Miss Lily is old, but she's quite strong, don't you think?"

"I guess so."

"Well, then," Clara said, as if that settled the matter for good.

Presently, Miss Olivia came down the stairs, a small bag in her hand. She looked more—normal now, Alma thought. Her hair was in place, face washed, a crisp blue dress under her grey cardigan. But she had forgotten her beads. She forced a smile.

"Alma, if you wouldn't mind, could you collect Miss Lily's reading glasses and her book from her study? They're on the table by the ashtray."

As her mother and Miss Olivia put on their coats, Alma ran down the hall and opened the study door. Without Miss Lily, the room's silence seemed unnaturally deep. The fireplace was cold, littered with grey ash, the desks in shadow, Miss Lily's chair empty and lifeless. Alma spotted the spectacles on the table beside a bookmarked copy of *Emma*. Jane Austen was one of Miss Lily's favourites, Alma recalled. She took up the book and glasses, and as she turned toward the door, she caught sight of a stack of papers on the desk. A buff-coloured envelope lay across the papers at an angle, covering the middle of the page. On the envelope was typed a name and address that Alma recognized immediately—RR Hawkins's publisher, Seabord Press.

Alma took a step nearer. Had Miss Lily written a new story? She read the bottom of the partly concealed page, easily making out the typed words "by RR Hawkins." Yes! she thought. It's true. RR Hawkins has broken her silence! Maybe I can be the first one to read it. If—when—Miss Lily gets out of the hospital, I'll ask her.

Then Alma's eyes rose to the top of the page above the envelope, and the words "THE DREAM-ARY."

She froze. It couldn't be, she told herself. There must be an explanation. Perhaps Miss Lily borrowed my title. That must be it. She fell ill before she could tell me. That was the reason for the invitation to tea—to ask permission. Alma carefully lifted the envelope and title page.

" '*SAM-U-ELLLL!*'" she read.

"Alma! Hurry up!"

Alma dashed from the room, numb and confused, and ran down the hall, the spectacles and novel in her hands.

Twenty

The leaves of autumn blazed with glory, faded, and were swept away on chill, blustery winds. Winter crept slowly into Charlotte's Bight. It was mid-December before the first snow, a spiteful two-day storm that left the town frosty and white and shivering. Not until the middle of January were the two rivers frozen all the way across, thick enough to permit skating and pick-up hockey games in the places where the wind kept the ice clear of snow.

Alma had seen Miss Lily only twice by the time Christmas arrived, in the hospital, a dreary place soaked in the odour of disinfectant and a churchlike reverent silence that seemed to threaten rather than comfort. The author, struck down by a stroke, had looked frail, her body under the blankets thin and birdlike, her face collapsed and wan. She had not awakened either time, so Alma hadn't heard her voice since that day in the park, so long ago.

Once, when Alma was walking with her mother along the harbour on a windy spring day, the water had captured her attention. The river's current swept powerfully into the harbour, but the wind, blowing at gale force in the opposite direction, built high, choppy white-caps and whipped foam into the air. It was as if the waters in the estuary wanted to rush in two directions at once.

The commotion that had churned in Alma's mind since that day in Miss Lily's empty study was like the contrary waters of the harbour.

Alma had said nothing to anyone about finding "The Dream-ary" with Miss Lily's name on the cover—"by RR Hawkins." She knew that to tell was to accuse. But, in keeping her secret, she could not ask for help or share her torment. There *must* be an explanation, she kept telling herself.

Alma was beginning to learn the trouble-some nature of secrets. You tucked them away in your mind, because you couldn't possibly think about them all day long, and you carried them with you. A secret was always there. There were some secrets that would fly out of the shadows, making your spirit soar when you remembered them. Others shambled into the light and snarled like an angry bear, and you shook with fear as you tried to shoo them away.

This secret was the worst kind, because it wasn't a fact. It was a question. Had RR Hawkins taken Alma's story? One answer made Alma burn with shame for misjudging her friend. The other filled her with sadness.

RR Hawkins, Miss Lily, was her friend. She liked being with Alma—the strolls to the park and harbour, the long Saturday-afternoon chats in the study, with the fire crackling and steam rising from the teacups. She had forgiven Alma for revealing her identity to Miss McAllister and the class. She had paid Alma's wages even on those few days when Alma turned up at the Chenoweth house to find there were no letters to copy. She had introduced Alma to calligraphy and who knew how many books. Miss Lily would never do anything against Alma.

And yet Alma was unable to put aside the

notion that RR Hawkins, desperate to write again, had taken "The Dream-ary," intending to publish it under her own name. Hadn't she praised the tale more than once? Miss Lily would never compliment something just to be polite. She didn't do anything just to be polite. It was one of the things Alma had grown to like about her. And hadn't Miss Lily, that day in the park when she talked about the passion to write, hinted that she wished she could regain the passion? Did she think that "The Dream-ary" was a ticket back to the world of writing? How could she take my story? Alma would ask herself, near tears, when she temporarily chose this explanation.

Was this why Miss Lily had fallen ill? Had she been overcome by guilt? Oh, what's the answer? Alma asked herself a thousand times. The question harried her, chasing her this way and that like a frightened rabbit.

Miss Olivia had asked Alma to continue coming to the house twice a week to help her tidy and dust and mop. Alma had wanted to refuse, uncomfortable with the idea, but she felt she couldn't. And as the winter wore on, the doubts Alma held slowly but inexorably overcame her faith in her stricken friend.

It's the only explanation that makes sense, Alma concluded one day at the beginning of March. RR Hawkins took—stole—my story.

Twenty-one

Spring came early that year, and by the end of May, Mr. Strachan had begun to hold physical education class in the schoolyard—baseball, volleyball and relay races. Alma was receiving good marks and stood second in her class, right behind Louise Arsenault, who, against all expectations, both hers and Alma's, had become Alma's friend. They discovered they both loved Conan Doyle's Sherlock Holmes stories—Louise bragged that she had read all of them except *The Sign of the Four*. Alma had read that one the year before, but kept the fact to herself. The two new friends even wrote a mystery together, with only a few arguments about what should happen when. It turned out, Alma discovered, that Louise wasn't such a snob after all.

Clara had, over the winter, shown her leadership skill in the kitchen and dining room of the Liffey, and now administered the restaurant side of things while Conor ran the bar. "And don't we make a great team," Clara had told Alma when she announced the news of her promotion over a pasta dinner at the Fireside Café. "He knows nothing about food and I know less about drink." Alma looked forward to the end of school when, her mother had promised, the two of them would take a trip, and stay with Alma's father's sister in Halifax.

One Saturday in the middle of June, Alma sat on a bench in the park by the estuary, writing in a notebook with her fountain pen. The soft afternoon air was suffused with the fragrance of daffodils and tulips and iris, and salt water. Occasionally she looked up toward the clouds that were building above the horizon as the afternoon wore on, as if searching for something, then she bent to her writing again, putting down the word she had been looking for.

"Amma," she heard.

Alma turned and smiled at the elderly woman sitting by the bench in a wheelchair, a dark shawl over her shoulders and thin woollen gloves on her hands, despite the warmth of the day.

"Yes, Miss Lily?" Alma replied, intent on the dark eyes sunken into Miss Lily's wrinkled face. The turned-down mouth twitched. The eyes looked skyward. Alma followed Miss Lily's line of sight. "Yes, I see it," she said.

Above the estuary, a bald eagle soared on motionless wings, riding the wind, like the point of a nib, Alma thought, writing with invisible ink on the dome of the sky.

Her face expressionless, Miss Lily seemed not to acknowledge Alma's words. The stroke had left some paralysis. Though she could stand, even take a few steps, Miss Lily had lost most of the use of her right leg. Her right arm was completely paralyzed. But worse, she had lost the ability to speak anything more than a few single-syllable utterances.

It seemed especially cruel to Alma that a fiercely intelligent woman whose gift was the talent to spin stories and express them in magical words could no longer communicate on anything above a basic level. But Alma understood her. Miss Lily's eyes still sparkled with energy, and behind them her mind was sharp and active.

When Miss Lily had come home from hospital and begun her long convalescence, Olivia Chenoweth had asked for Alma's help, after first clearing it with Alma's mother. So Alma's job had changed once again. She no longer copied letters or did light housekeeping; she was companion to Miss Lily, visiting at least twice a week. People who wrote to RR Hawkins now received a form letter stating that the author was convalescing from an illness and unable to answer personally.

At first, Alma hadn't wanted to return to the Chenoweth house. Though she had wished RR Hawkins the best, and hoped she'd recover from her stroke, Alma hadn't wanted to be with her. But she found she couldn't say no. No matter what Miss Lily had done, Alma couldn't abandon her, especially after Miss Olivia had pressed her, explaining how much she needed help with her mother, and how she just knew in her heart that Alma's presence would help Miss Lily get better. How can I refuse? Alma had asked herself. Didn't Miss Lily forgive me in the past?

And then, at the end of April, everything had become clear.

"Man-core," Miss Lily said.

"Are you sure, Miss Lily? We've been to see the display twice this week."

"Man-core."

Alma smiled and got up from the bench and put her notebook in the bag that hung from the handles of the wheelchair. She tucked the woollen blanket around Miss Lily's legs and adjusted the shawl so that it covered her useless arm. Miss Lily smiled at her with her eyes.

Walking slowly, Alma pushed the wheelchair up Little Wharf Road to Grafton Street, then east, past the school, to a bookstore on the corner of Springwater Road and Church Street. Until recently, Alma had never gone there. At the Manticore, they sold only new books.

Alma stopped the wheelchair in front of the store window. "Oh, good, the display is still there," she said.

"Local Author" read a carefully lettered sign behind the glass. And beside the sign were stacks of books, some turned to face the window, so that passersby could see the covers. Alma recalled the day in Miss Lily's silent study when she had discovered the manuscript on the desk, with the envelope resting on top of it, and "by RR Hawkins" at the foot of the page. Now,

on the book cover, she read what she would
have seen if she had lifted the envelope:

The Dream-ary
by
Alma Neal

edited and with an introduction
by RR Hawkins

"Hum," RR Hawkins said.
"Yes, Miss Lily," Alma replied. "Let's go
home."

CHAPTER

Twenty-two

The next day, Alma and her mother sat down to a breakfast of eggs fried sunny side up, peameal bacon and toasted soda bread. Licking her lips, Alma broke her toast into bits and soaked up the runny egg yolks, savouring every piece. She then sliced the thick, pink bacon and the fried eggs into bite-size strips. One piece of bacon and one piece of egg together on the fork, then into her mouth they went.

"You've made eating breakfast an art form," Clara said, sipping her tea.

Alma nodded, munching happily.

When breakfast was over and the table cleared, Clara went into her bedroom and returned with a book in her hand. "Sit down,

please, Alma. You can finish the dishes later."
She placed the book on the table. "I'd like you
to sign this for me."

Alma sat in her chair, took up her pen and,
in her best calligraphy, wrote on the title page,
"To the best mom in the world, love, Alma."

"Mom, did you know all along?" she asked.

"That Sunday when Miss Lily fell ill," Clara
began, "the day she invited us to tea. I think she
intended to speak to you about sending your
story to her publisher. Later, when things had
settled down and Miss Lily was home again,
Miss Olivia mentioned it to me. I told her to go
ahead. We thought it would be a nice surprise."

Clara picked up the book and turned a few
pages. "Miss Lily wrote a lovely introduction,"
she said. "She says you have a gifted imagination."

"And she called me her special friend," Alma
said, straightening up in her chair.

Alma's mother handed her the book. "Read
it to me," she said.

Alma took the book and opened it. And,
with her mother smiling and looking proudly
on, she began.

"'The Dream-ary,'" she read, "'by Alma Neal.'"

CHAPTER ONE

"SAM-U-ELLLL!"

Uh-oh, Sammy thought.

"Young man, you just take a good look behind you!"

Careful not to spill any water from the glass fishbowl in his hands, the fishbowl that contained no fish, Sammy hunched up his shoulders and bent down his head, the way he always did when he found himself in trouble. He turned slowly and looked behind him.

Across his mother's freshly cleaned and polished kitchen floor were twelve splotchy, grimy brown boot prints. Sammy swallowed hard and looked down at his boots and saw not leather but mud. Mud clotted on the soles, mud spattered on the toes, mud soaked into the laces. He had been so careful not to spill any (slightly smelly) water from the bowl where his frogs' eggs had just that morning hatched into little black wiggly pollywogs, that he'd forgotten about his boots.

"Sorry, Mom," he said. "I'll clean it up right away."

So as not to make things worse, Sammy decided to kick off his boots, but the left one stuck. He kicked harder, sloshing slightly stinky water down his pants onto the freshly washed and polished floor. He kicked a third time and sent his boot flying across the kitchen. It slammed into a cupboard door, leaving a brown splotch, and fell right into Scout's bowl, sending hundreds of chunks of puppy kibble rolling across the floor.

"Oh, shoot!" Sammy exclaimed. He took a step—and put his stockinged foot down into the puddle of frog-water he had just spilled. His foot slid ever so slowly away from him, like a bar of soap on a shower floor, until Sammy found himself doing the splits. When his bum hit the linoleum the shock bounced the bowl out of his hands and up into the air, where it seemed to hang for a split second before it descended to Sammy's outstretched knee, thumped him painfully, rolled to the floor, cracked into exactly eighteen pieces, and flooded the shiny linoleum with slightly smelly water, rotted weeds and grass and—Sammy knew this because he had counted them only five minutes before—a hundred and seven wriggling pollywogs.

Sammy knew he was done for. His mom stood in the doorway between the kitchen and the dining room where she had been setting the table. (Sammy's grandparents, all four of them, were coming over for dinner.) Her hands were crossed over her chest. Sammy was sure he could see steam coming from her ears as she started to yell. He hunched up his shoulders again, sitting helplessly in a small lake of stinky water, surrounded by dog food and leaping pollywogs.

After Sammy's mother had finished telling him off (it took her a long time, and she wouldn't let Sammy help her clean the floor) he went to his room to listen to music.

"No record player!" his mother yelled.

So he began to flip through a magazine.

"No magazines!" came his mother's voice from the kitchen.

Sammy turned on the radio. Maybe there was a ball game on. He kept the volume so low he could hardly hear it.

"No radio!"

Sammy threw himself onto his bed. It wasn't fair, he thought. He hadn't meant to mess up his mother's floor. Or to chase Scout through his father's geraniums (and tulips and poppies and pansies) yesterday. Or to park his bike against the back bumper of the car the day before that. After all, *he* hadn't backed the car over his bike. And he hadn't *meant* to leave his baseball glove out in the rain last week. He hadn't *known* that balancing an egg on the end of his nose wasn't a good idea. (It had taken his father eight and a half minutes to scrape the yellow goo from the rug in his room. Sammy knew. He had been standing in the corner, facing the clock.)

No, it wasn't fair. His mom and dad were too hard on him. I'll bet, Sammy thought, his face hot with frustration, they didn't even want to have me. Bet I was an accident or something, he pouted. Bet I was adopted. Bet they found me in a cardboard box on the front porch one day and they had to keep me. They didn't have any choice. There was a law or something.

I'll show them, he thought. I'll make them sorry.

CHAPTER TWO

Sammy lived seven blocks from his school. To get there, he walked, usually with Meredith, along a street lined with tall maple trees.

Between his house and the school was the library.

Sammy loved the library. It stood back from the street, and a wide sidewalk led to its tall oak doors with shiny brass rails slanting across them. As soon as he was old enough, his father had taken him to get his first library card. It had his name and address on it.

Soon Sammy knew his way around the bookshelves. He knew that an F on a book meant it was a story, a 9-something meant it was a true story about someone's life, 638 was bees. Sammy knew where the magazines stood in wooden racks, and where the story corner was. He went to the story corner every Saturday morning to hear the librarian read from the books.

On the Saturday morning after Sammy had decided that his parents hadn't ever wanted to have a baby (him), he went to the library on his own. But as soon as he got to the story corner, he had to go to the bathroom. He made his way down the stairs and into the dimly lit basement, feeling a little bit creepy because it smelled damp and the light wasn't good. He saw a door, opened it, and realized he was outside, facing a set of steps that led upwards.

The door clicked shut behind him. And locked itself.

Uh-oh, Sammy thought, I can't get back in!

He went up the steps and found himself in a narrow, sunny street. The road was paved with smooth stones and lined with narrow shops. Wish Street, read the sign.

Most of the shop doors stood open, and the odour of chocolate, freshly baked soda bread, hot buttered popcorn and other delicacies filled the air. Across the street the bakery window was packed with cakes and loaves and bins of candies. Beside it was a toy store with a red-and-white candy-striped pole in front. And there wasn't one fish-and-chip shop to be seen.

At the end of the street was a shabby shop no bigger than Sammy's garage. In the window was an antique spinning wheel coated with dust, with cobwebs looped between the spokes. On the sign above the closed door, ancient letters with curly flourishes spelled out "Dream-ary."

Feeling completely lost by now, Sammy hesitantly went in, causing a little bell above him to tinkle. He looked at his watch. It was 11:30 on the dot. I'm missing story time, and I have to be back by 12:00, he reminded himself. The shop was filled with row upon row of cases. The walls were lined to the ceiling with shelves. A gallery stretched along the walls, with ladders from the floor to the gallery and from there to the ceiling. The shelves and tables were laden with wooden boxes, and the boxes were stuffed with cards with writing on them.

"Hello there!" someone shouted. "Welcome to the Dream-ary, yesyes. My name is Clio."

The voice, which sounded a little like a fingernail scratched on paper, came from behind one of the ladders. Out popped a very small, very thin, very old woman, with pure white hair and a face laced with kindly wrinkles and a gap between her two front teeth. She was wearing a flower-print dress and work boots and a baseball cap. A pencil rested behind one ear.

"Hello," Sammy replied, looking around and wondering how many hundreds of boxes the shop contained, and how many thousands of cards. "Um," he faltered, "what's a dream-ary?"

"Well," the woman said in her scratchy voice that seemed much too big for such a small person, "you've heard of an apiary, haven't you? Or a dictionary, yesyes? Or an aviary. Or a . . . Or how about a dromed-ary—nono, that's a camel, nevermind. How about a library? Heard of that, yesyes?"

"Of course," Sammy said.

"Well, then, you know that *liber* in Latin means book, so a liber-ary is a place where you find books, yesyes, and a diction-ary is a place to find words yesyes, so a dream-ary is a place to find . . . ?"

"Er, dreams?" Sammy tried.

"Clever boy." The woman beamed. "Here, instead of borrowing books to read, you borrow dreams to dream."

Sammy frowned. How could a dream be borrowed?

"No bad dreams, mind," Clio broke in on his thoughts. "No nightmares. Nonono. We have daydreams and nighttime dreams, sweet dreams and pipe dreams. On almost every topic, yesyes," she added, throwing wide her arms. "We have toy dreams, fun dreams, dessert dreams, sports dreams, pet dreams. Why not borrow one?"

Sammy scanned the boxes on the nearest table. He saw no numbers on them like those on the books in the library, just words.

"Well . . .," he said, not quite sure what to do.

"Wonderful," Clio exclaimed, evidently certain Sammy had said yes. "What would you like, whatwhat?"

Sammy's stomach chose that moment to growl as loud as a polar bear. He had eaten no breakfast and he was hungry.

"All right, food it is, yesyes!" Clio said, and before Sammy's unbelieving eyes she dashed to a ladder, scrambled up to the gallery, clumped sideways a few feet in her thick boots and turned to him. "Dessert, I suppose," she offered.

"All right," Sammy said. "That sounds great."

In a blink, Clio pulled a box from the shelf, extracted a red envelope, scooted back down the ladder and handed it to Sammy.

"Just put it under your pillow when you go to bed," she said. "It's due back in one week. And," she added, knitting her thick white brows and wagging her finger very close to Sammy's nose, "you must never forget to sign the dream card inside the envelope before you put it under your pillow, nevernever."

"Goodbye, and thank you," Sammy said on his way out the door, after Clio had given him directions back to the library.

"Bye-bye, nevermind," said Clio.

Sammy found the library door easily. He looked at his watch again. It was 11:30. That's funny, he thought. My watch must have stopped working. And the door was no longer locked.

CHAPTER THREE

Sammy could hardly wait to get to bed to see if the dream card really worked the way Clio said it would. So as soon as he had finished his arithmetic homework, he said goodnight to his mom and dad.

"What?" Dad exclaimed. "It's only 7:30."

Sammy looked at his watch. It was working again. It said 7:30.

"Are you feeling sick?" Mom asked, a look of concern on her face. "Come here and let me feel your forehead."

"No, I'm feeling fine," Sammy said. "Honest. I'm tired."

His parents exchanged curious glances as Sammy climbed the stairs. In his room, he quickly put on his pyjamas. He opened the big red envelope and removed the card from inside.

"It looks pretty ordinary to me," he said out loud.

The card was white, with faint blue lines on it, almost exactly like the ones Dad wrote recipes on. He had a whole box of them beside the stove. On the lines, people had signed their names and written the date. "Dylan," Sammy read, "April 26. Megan, November 30." And nearer the bottom of the first column, "Brendan, April 16."

Sammy hesitated before writing his name, for he was still doubtful, but he had promised. So he signed in black ink under the last name on the list with his favourite fountain pen.

He slipped the card under his pillow, climbed into bed, pulled up the covers and turned out the lamp. Squeezing his eyes shut, he tried to make himself go to sleep. But it wouldn't work. Thoughts marched around inside his mind, tramping up and down, making an awful racket. After a while, Sammy gave up trying to force himself to dream. And right away, he fell asleep.

And what a dream he had.

Sammy found himself, in his bathing suit, standing on a long, bouncy diving board made of licorice. He jounced once, then plunged into a lake of sweet dark chocolate. He didn't need to open his mouth—he could taste through his skin as he swam on his back. He came to an island mounded high with pineapples, man-goes and plums, peaches and cherries, oranges and tangerines, grapes and raspberries. Sammy crawled from the lake onto a beach of granulated sugar. He bathed in cola, then ginger ale, then root beer, all the while tasting, tasting, through every pore. He slid down a slippery chute of toffee, landing in a bin of whipped cream. He ran along a nougat road, skidded through strawberry jam, and bumped into a table loaded with cakes, custards and pastries, tarts and jellies, flans and puddings, eclairs and turnovers and doughnuts.

In the morning, Sammy reluctantly got out of bed. In the bathroom mirror, he noticed a smudge of caramel frosting on his lip. He licked it off. It tasted good.

"Sammy! Breakfast!" his mother called up to him.

"Not today, Mom," he said. "I'm not hungry."

&

CHAPTER FOUR

Sammy was in trouble again.

Over the past weeks, Sammy had visited the Dream-ary every Saturday morning. It was easy, because as soon as he passed through the door at the end of the dark hall in the library basement, time stood still. He could take as long as he wanted to choose a dream. When he returned to the library, no one even knew he had been gone.

One day after school let out, Sammy had raced home on his bike, shooting down the street, swooping into the driveway as fast as he could without losing control. As he approached the garage's double door he thought, Mom and Dad will be happy that I remembered to put my bike away. He carefully aimed the bike to pass exactly between his dad's new car and the garage wall.

But.

He had forgotten the carrier his dad had mounted on the bike behind his seat.

The carrier that held his backpack.

The carrier that was a little bit wider than his handlebars.

Screeeeeeeeee!

Now Sammy waited in his room while his mom and dad decided how to punish him. He didn't have to wait long.

"Sammy! Come down here," his mother called.

"Now!" added his father.

Sammy stood in the kitchen before his parents, whose faces were dark and stern, whose arms were crossed on their chests, whose mouths were turned down at the corners.

"No more bicycle!" said his mother.

"Come home right after school every day and stay home," commanded his father.

"But—," Sammy tried.

"No buts!" said both of his parents together.

It was two weeks before Sammy got permission to go to the library again. He walked along the street on Saturday morning, kicking a can along the gutter, gloomy and grumpy.

Bet my grandparents didn't treat them like that, Sammy thought. Bet my parents wish they could get rid of me. Bet they never wanted me, he concluded, not for the first time.

In the Dream-ary, Sammy passed row on row of boxes. "Sports." "Treats." "Friends." Tried them already, he said to himself. "Hobbies." "Pets." He couldn't decide what to borrow today. Maybe I'll borrow desserts again, he decided. He knew exactly where to find the box. It was up a ladder to the gallery and along a bit.

But as he walked down the row, he brushed against an overloaded table, sending a box crashing to the floor.

"What noise was that, whatwhatwhat?" called Clio from high atop a ladder at the back of the shop.

"Er, nothing," Sammy replied, picking up the envelopes and stuffing them back into the box as quickly as he could. But one card had slipped from its envelope and flipped underneath the table. Sammy meant to leave it where it had fallen, but he decided that would be rude, so he got down on his knees, crawled through the thick dust under the table, picked up the card and carefully, scrabbling backwards like a lobster, returned to the narrow aisle between the tables. He stood up.

And that was when he looked at the card. "CHILDREN" was stamped on the front.

Why would anyone want to dream about children? Sammy wondered. He turned the card over. There were lots of signatures, so many the card was almost full. Sammy noticed "125" on the top right-hand corner.

Wow, he thought. This is the 125th card for children dreams. The dessert card is only number 34. A lot of people wanted to dream about children. He ran his eye over the names.

And saw some writing he recognized.

His mother's name, and right beneath it, his father's. And their names were repeated. The dates showed that they had borrowed the card on many occasions—*before* Sammy was born.

Beginning where his heart was, Sammy felt a wonderful warm glow spread through him, and he said to himself, Mom and Dad *did* want me.

THE END

Alma closed the book and slowly turned it over in her hands. She ran her fingers along the spine and read the words on the cover once again. Her mother sat across the kitchen table from her, beaming with pride, the rope of lustrous chestnut hair resting on the threadbare collar of her dress.

"You know what, my girl?" Clara said.

"What, Mom?"

"I don't think you're twoderempty."

Acknowledgements

Thanks to Maya Mavjee for her support of this and other projects, to Meg Taylor for her enthusiastic and valued assistance, to John Pearce for his guiding hand and, as always, to Ting-xing Ye.

About the Author

William Bell is the award-winning author of eleven books for young people, including *Zack*, which won the Mr. Christie's Book Award, and *Stones*, which is a CLA YA Book of the Year. Bell lives in Orillia, Ontario, with writer Ting-xing Ye.

ALSO BY WILLIAM BELL

Stones

Garnet Havelock know what it's like to be on
the outside, not one of the crowd. Now, in his
final year of high school, he's just marking time,
waiting to get out into the real world.

Then a mysterious girl transfers to his school
and Garnet thinks he might have found the
woman of his dreams—if only he could get her
to talk to him.

At the same time, Garnet becomes caught up
in a mystery centred in his community. As he
and Raphaella draw closer to the truth, they
uncover a horrifying chapter in the town's history, and learn how deep-seated prejudices and
persecution from the past can still reverberate
in the present.

SEAL BOOKS / ISBN: 0-7704-2875-4

ALSO BY WILLIAM BELL

Zack

Uprooted by his parents' move to the outskirts of a small Ontario town, friendless and at the lowest point of his life, Zack undertakes research into the life of Richard Pierpoint, former African slave, soldier of the American Revolution as well as the War of 1812, and the pioneer farmer who cleared the land on which Zack's house now stands. Pierpoint's story inspires Zack to go to Mississippi to look for his maternal grandfather. What Zack discovers shakes the foundation of all he once believed.

SEAL BOOKS / ISBN: 0-7704-2860-6

ALSO BY WILLIAM BELL

Forbidden City

Seventeen-year-old Alex Jackson is thrilled when his father, a cameraman with the Canadian Broadcasting Corporation, asks Alex to join him on assignment in China. Not only will he get some time off from school, but Alex, who is a Chinese history buff, knows this trip is the chance of a lifetime.

Alex and his dad could not have predicted that they would get caught up in the historic events that begin to sweep China in the spring of 1989. As students and civilians demonstrate for democracy in Tian An Men Square, Alex experiences the thrill of being a reporter. However, his excitement turns to horror and dismay as the movement becomes violent. Alex and his father know they must communicate the story to the rest of the world, but at what cost to their own lives?

SEAL BOOKS / ISBN: 0-7704-2813-4